SOUNDS FROM THE SOUL

My journey into Love

Sounds from the Soul – My journey into Love
By Sissel Adronia
Original titel: Sjelens Toner - reisen inn i kjærlighet (2021)
Copyright © Sissel Adronia Karlsen 2024
www.adroniaslight.com

Cover: Juan Antonio Alamo
Mentor: Eva Andrea
Translator: Maryanne Berg-Hansen
Editor: Debbie Allen
Layout: Luisa van Erven
Publisher: BoD - Books on Demand, Oslo, Norway
Print: BoD - Books on Demand, Norderstedt, Germany
ISBN: 978-82-845-1035-4

Sounds from the Soul
My journey into Love

"A beautiful book, beautifully written and it goes straight to the heart. It is a book about another dimension, of deep love and unity. It leaves a deep impression that gives afterthoughts and contemplation for yourself. Life becomes a before and after, reading this book."

Anna Margrethe S. Bergvoll, author and Gestalt therapist

"Reading the book gave me renewed faith that my own journey is also important and right, and reassurance that I am not alone in having these thoughts and challenges."

Iver Daatland, journalist

"I see the book as a tool in, for example, women's circles. It raises so many nice questions that invite sharing. It provokes and promotes a limited perception of the world. The book invites courage. Courage to listen inwardly, courage to step out, courage to share, and above all courage to be honest."

Helle True, storyteller

"This is one of the most energetically powerful books I have read. It is as if the energy of God passes into the heart and creates deep recognition at the soul level. The story is like a medicine drink that goes far into the reader's subconscious and soul. I close the book feeling that I have been touched by angels and held in the most beautiful divine embrace."

Eva Andrea, author and spiritual teacher

Thanks

For this book to be a finished result, some people have been particularly important. Every part of life has its significance, but I want to give recognition to those who have contributed to this story which is now coming out into the public domain.

First and foremost, I want to thank my children. By choosing me as their mother, I honoured the love of knowing from an unconditional reservoir. They made me bring out a strength I didn't know I had, and have contributed with their love and acceptance of me as who I am.

I also want to thank my parents as they are the direct cause of me being here in this world. It is also through them, and their stories, that I gained the experiences I was meant to have. At the same time, I would also like to thank my children for the unity we have always had and still have. Although we are different by nature, we have profound respect for each other and the love between us is strong. Thank you for always being here.

I would not be where I am today without the help of my skilled and loving shamans. Thank you very much Ynes, David, Laura, Lila, and José. There have been several others with you at times, but you are like family to me. I am eternally grateful for the help in removing the wilderness that had grown large and powerful around me. To find my home I needed the wisdom you imparted.

A big thank you to my mentor Eva Andrea, for her steady guidance through the process. You challenged me to be as open as I am in the book, and you strengthened my belief that it is possible to say things as they are. With your help I found the courage to express my voice. Thank you!

English is not my langue, so it was important to find someone reading through the translation. Through magic coincidence I was guided to the most perfect woman I could encounter. Thank you, Debbie, for all your work and good advice to make this the best book it could be. I'm so grateful for your effort and lovely presence, I couldn't find anyone better than you!

There have been many people cheering me on in this process, who have backed me up and contributed their faith in the product that was created. Thank you so much to all of you. You know who you are.

On this path
effort never goes to waste,
and there is no failure.
Even a little effort
toward spiritual awareness
will protect you
from the greatest fear.

The Bhagavad Gita

Prologue

For the last few months, the voice inside me has been pounding harder and more often. Something is pulling and the uneasiness increases. I know what it is all about. The soul contract before I got into this physical life is going to be fulfilled: to share my healing-journey. The book is going to be written and the right time is approaching fast. It has been on hold for years as if it were to mature. I needed to mature, and now I know that the time is close. I have put it off for a long time, but now it is like I can't push it in front of me anymore. It is a certainty that I cannot move forward until this step is done. The life behind me has been like an adventurous journey, a story to be shared. When I felt the certainty sink in, I made an appointment with my higher self; I promised that I would write the book if I found a mentor who could walk beside me and mentor me in this difficult task. The book wouldn't be an ordinary one, I was to open my inside and show it to the world. Scary! It took two weeks. The creative web of synchronicity that the universe weaves never cease to amaze me. Magically and upon sudden impulses she was introduced to my life: Eva Andrea. It couldn't be just anyone that was obvious, it had to be someone who knew what I wanted to convey. When she showed up, I knew in an instant that it was right, my intuition told me so.

During our first conversation she asked me to do a meditation after we finished our meeting, to bring me in touch with the result. That same evening, I settled into the meditation which she had sent to me, closed my eyes and put on headphones to stop all outside noises. I disappeared deep into my soul as the voice guided me on the journey. The book appeared at the end, it was lit up with shooting stars splashing out of it like fireworks, the range of colours was fascinating against the deep blue night sky that surrounded the book. The voice stopped, but I wasn't ready to finish so I asked if those who were going to guide me in the writing would come forward. The scene shifted. Now I was walking in the highlands, a place well known to me as it has appeared in many meditations and dreams. The grass is brown and short, no vegetation is to be seen, just high mountains rising in front of me, I sense wide views on both sides as if it is in a mountain pass. On the peaks I see the snow sparkling in the sun and I can feel that the air is clear and crisp, the breeze on my face is sweet, but not cold. A river flows through the area dividing the terrain in two parts. I walk with firm steps in the direction towards it.

I approach the riverbank and sit down. I stick my feet into the water, and I can feel how the water flows quietly between my toes and that it reaches to the middle of my calves. It is as clear as crystal, the bottom of the river is covered with stones in varied sizes. I become aware that I am not alone anymore, and I look up and I see two people walking towards me. As they approach, I recognise Jesus and Mother Mary. They stop a short distance from the riverbank, and I look at them standing side by side without uttering a word. Their gaze is direct, and I feel that they have come to attend the meeting between me and my guides. Then I see three men in monk's robes approaching and they stop right next to the riverbank. I recognise Rumi and Shakespeare, but I must ask who is the last one. It is John of the Cross; the name comes flowing towards me. I am laughing at the fact that they want to help me in my task, it was totally unexpected.

We talk for a while, Jesus and Mary are still quiet, but their presence is strong. After the conversation I look down at my feet and the stones where they are resting are now far, far away. It is like looking through a portal and I know that it is Mother Earth I see deep down. I notice that the stones are shaped by the water floating constantly where it polishes the sharp edges, I can see that they now have become round and smooth. I know that each stone signifies the burden everyone is carrying, the weight of pain through the loss of connection with themselves and their souls. I look up and notice that I am alone. I get up and stroll back to where I came from, now I am ready to do the work. I know it is going to be tough, what I am going to tell exists beyond words and in between thoughts. The help I need to convey the language I don't have is in place, and I am making myself vulnerable to both ridicule and mockery, but I know that all is good. The strength which I have acquired through my experiences is strong enough to endure those who don't understand. I know who I am and that is enough. I am ready to embark on the next chapter of my journey.

Total Emptiness

I almost ran out of the assembly hall. The last hour had been one of the hardest and most confusing I had ever experienced, and I couldn't get out fast enough. The room I fled from was packed with people. "The Troubadors" were very popular and were always playing for a full house. Tonight, there were probably two hundred people attending the concert, as many as the venue could fit. I made myself as small and invisible as I could as I hurried towards the exit. The door I saw in front of me was my rescue and I breathed a sigh of relief when pressing the handle down. What I had experienced during the last hour I didn't want to experience ever again, I only wanted to go home. The fresh air felt like balm on my face, I was safe. The sun was setting, shining its rays against the treetops with its orange light as I peeked out into freedom. Autumn was about to make its entrance and nature's beautiful colours were enhanced by the golden light.

I felt as though my blood was freezing in my veins, what was happening? The relief and joy I had expected to flow through me hadn't come. There were no feelings, not even a tiny sign, it was empty. I looked around and spotted my car: it was going to take me home, I thought, as I slowly began to walk towards it. I could think and act on my thoughts, they were swirling around in my head to see if I could grasp what was happening. Confused, I entered the car. This was absurd, how can everything that is me disappear in one moment? I was transformed into a living robot, an empty shell where everything inside had disappeared. The thoughts were there, I could analyse and rationalise, but everything I identified as me was no more, the body was just a vessel of bones and blood acting on intentions and will. Where was I?

The surroundings were the same as when I had arrived an hour and a half earlier, but everything had changed. I started on my way home to put the kids to bed, they were my excuse for not being able to attend the whole concert. My friend stayed behind, but luckily, I had only promised to be there for an hour, and I was able to sneak out. It had been the hardest hour that I could recall. How was this possible? I was almost thirty-three years old and had had many strange experiences, but this was beyond anything I had ever heard or read about. My mind wandered backwards as the traffic slowly moved forward, I tried to find the feelings of being me by using my memory, but I could not. The void screamed at me as if my inner self had been laid to sleep, I was a body with a head that could think, period.

The day had started like any other day this Thursday early in September 1991. Nothing had prepared me for the fact that before the end of the day my whole existence would have turned around. Life would forever be termed as before and after what was about to happen. For the past five years I had been alone with my two children and life was tough. When I married, I was a nineteen-year-old young girl, education was opted out of, in favour of family life. The weekdays after the divorce had therefore passed in evening school to finish the subjects which I needed to apply for colleges, work during the day, and to take care of the kids. I had finished the subjects I needed, but I hadn't decided what to choose as a profession. This evening I had envisioned as a pleasant element in my busy life, an evening with singing and music.

What happened had scared the hell out of me and now I was on my way home more confused than ever. To prevent fear from taking over my mind I began to wander backwards in time. After years of focussing on gathering the courage to get out of the marriage, I was left without an education, without a job, and a huge debt. The reason I had married so young was a desperate bid to find love. The last few years of living with my parents had been filled with bickering and discussions between them, and both sought support for their views. Several times my mother took huge overdoses of sedatives or was bedridden. We moved to Spain when I was sixteen years old, and there she could buy the drugs she wanted. I often lay in my bed at night listening to the bickering, anxious that my little sister would wake up and get scared. The big pinecones which my mother picked on her walks I often heard banging on the walls downstairs. All the turmoil and chaos lead me to wanting to escape to some faraway place and never come back.

Now I was on the run again, this time from something I didn't understand. When my friend had persuaded me to join the concert I had said yes, but only for an hour. I wasn't interested in religious gatherings, even though I had my childhood faith, and this event was organised by a religious group, she, on the other hand, was looking for a church where she could belong. We had many lively discussions where we exchanged thoughts and opinions within my biggest field of interest: life and death. Our different angles were rewarding, her references from the bible and mine from metaphysical books. I had found books of the Seth material, and I was on fire over all truths that resonated with my way of thinking. The Seth material is a series of books in which Jane Roberts channelled an otherworldly spirit named Seth, in the period from 1963 until her death in 1984, and they became termed as a cornerstone of the new-age philosophy. My friend disagreed with my choice of literature and kept trying to drag me along to meetings whilst I wanted to avoid them. When I was empty of arguments to avoid going this evening, I had capitulated and so I had joined this night's concert.

My friends mother came in the afternoon to babysit, and when dinner was done, I left my daughter there, as my son wanted to stay with friends. Our girls were the same age and loved playing together, so the argument that I lacked a babysitter was not valid. We arrived some minutes before the concert started and people poured in. The hall filled up quickly, and we ended up in the middle of the congregation. They began to play, one person on the piano and the other with a guitar. Already during the first song I felt the tears pressing behind my eyes, both the lyrics and the music went straight into my heart. Instantly I felt how the words penetrated my heart, as if it had collapsed the wall I had built up through years of suffering. I didn't know how to keep the tears inside and I clenched my hands together in my lap. I hardly dared to breathe out of fear my crying would come out as convulsive crying.

The words spoke directly to my heart. They revealed everything which I had kept deep inside and locked so far away that even I couldn't notice the pain and loneliness that was stored, feelings I didn't consciously know of. I couldn't understand how it was possible to elicit such a reaction only through a song. I would not break down in the middle of a crowd, whilst the only thing I felt the need to do was to lie down on the floor, curl up and let all my despair out. I closed my eyes firmly and tried as best as I could to shut the emotions down.

During the struggle to stay gathered and united, I felt an energy circulating around me. I knew it wanted to enter, but in this situation, I kept it away. This is a suggestion, I thought, and I certainly didn't want to honour that. I felt the urge to get up and steer away, and if we hadn't been in the middle of the row with a lot of people on each side, I think I might have run away. The promise I had given to my friend also held me in place, so I was stuck fighting the tears which wanted to come out and the energy that wanted to get in.

As I was driving home nothing wanted to get either in nor out, everything was quiet and empty except for a jumble of thoughts. Once home I was able to perform all the rituals as normal, supper, chatting, and reading for my youngest daughter in bed. It was always good to end the day listening to all they had to share from their experiences, but this evening I couldn't be completely present. When both were in bed, I sat down in my living room to think about the strange phenomenon I had experienced. When will *I* be back? I sat in silence and waited, but nothing happened, the stillness was complete. After a while fear tried to sneak in: what if I was gone forever? The fear crawled up my back by the thought. I am probably back tomorrow when I wake up, I thought to comfort myself. I turned off the lights, locked the doors, and finished my nightly bathroom routine in a hurry to get to sleep as quickly as possible. I got into bed and pulled the covers well over me. What happened next changed my life forever.

Immersed in Love

As soon as I pulled the duvet over my body, I felt the energy from earlier come around me again. This time it came with a deep knowing that it was God. Now that I was lying at home in my own bed, everything was calm and there was no one around, a clarity entered me along with the knowing that it was God. There was no room for doubt, and I knew that I had a choice, it was up to me to allow this energy to enter my body or not. The last few hours of myself being absent swept through my mind; I couldn't live a life that way, it would only be existence without living. The thought made me terrified, so I said with anxiety in my mind: You better come in then.

The moment that I gave permission, a force started to enter inside me from the soles of my feet and began its movements upwards. It came in waves and was surging with a force that would have knocked me over had I been upright. It went up my calves and continued through the pelvis, abdomen, chest, back, arms, neck, and head. I was left paralysed as it drifted through my whole body again and again. It was like a tidal flood washing over me, and I could feel how it cleansed all my cells one by one. I have never felt such a force either before or since, and have never been so conscious of every cell in my body. It felt as if everything inside the cells was renewed, the contents were switched from dead to living organisms. I felt the cells awakening one by one while the waves washed through them again and again. Without being able to move a finger I just registered how each one of them came back to life, I can't explain it in any other way. Even thirty years after the experience it is like I am there experiencing it all anew as I write, it becomes alive again as if the time between does not exist.

After all the cells were filled with new life, the waves died down. I thought it was over and took a deep breath as if I had been holding it, but I didn't even finish the outbreath before it started all over again. It started the same way, but now the force was made of love. This love had a fullness and a richness in it that cannot be described, like an ecstasy multiplied by a thousand. It bounced through me again and again like a tidal wave with no end. Each cell was filled with this love as if it were leaving itself behind. I just knew that this was not something created, this love is what it has always been and always will be. Without a doubt I knew that this was the substance I was made of, that we all are made of, and that which gives life. All life is created in this power of love, and it is from this substance that all life emerges, not just humans, all life is inside this and created by it.

When my freshly cleansed cells were filled in abundance by this joyful ecstasy, a vision opened. I was shown how the force gushed out of my heart and filled the room I was lying in before it spread outwards. The whole house was enclosed or existed inside this force. I could see my children sleeping in it, the force was inside them, and they were in it, it looked like everything in the house existed in a living wave. It continued enveloping the garden, the grass, the rocks, the fence, the neighbours, nothing existed outside of the force of love. I saw how it spread to the whole neighbourhood where my ex-husband lived. He did everything he could to thwart the visitor agreement we had committed to about the children, and he refused to cooperate so that I could work one night a week. It had led to many difficulties which could have been avoided. Even he was in this love, and it was okay. It was just how it was, and I knew that all was fine. I was shown how the force of love extended beyond and enveloped the city I lived in, the country, the continent, and the whole world, it was in everything that existed, nothing was outside of it.

Here existed stones, trees, houses, people, and animals, and I saw myself smaller than a little grain of sand, but I still had the same power as the one I felt washing through me. This was the substance that bound it all together, and it consisted of pure love. I knew that this was God, it wasn't something I wondered or assumed; this was pure full assurance. When I saw the stream flooding out from my heart and finally covering the entire globe, it was shown as a kind of fog-like, white matter, but completely transparent. It was around everything that is, and it was inside everything that is, everything was included, or rather everything existed *in* it. As I laughed inside me at what was being shown, I felt all my worries fading away. All that was important, all that was true, was this existence of pure love: period. When this force covered the entire earth and began to ascend towards the universe, the vision disappeared, and the waves stopped. A complete silence surrounded me.

I was left lying in my bed looking at the ceiling. Everything in me was silent: total silence. Even the thoughts were absent. A tiny feeling swept around; what happened? What was this? There were no words to use, nothing I could compare it to. I was left with a feeling of being - forever - always. There was no time. The body, the bed I was lying in, the world that I lived in, everything was just there. Peace. Never had I experienced such all-consuming *peace*. I wanted to be here forever, consumed by it, and never leave. A door had opened that I hadn't known was closed, and I didn't want to leave this presence. Eventually I drifted into a kind of sleep.

The Voice of God

My first thought the next morning when I awoke was about what had happened last night whilst feeling the love vibrating as if my skin had come to life. I swung my legs out of bed and almost floated out of the room, it was like the floor had turned into cotton and I had wings which carried me forward. On my way to wake up the children to get them ready for school, I thought of how much I love them and abruptly stopped. Love poured out of my heart like a river. I had never experienced anything like it, as if the love that previously had come from my head as a thought, now came like a physical waterfall from my heart directly towards them. I could see the stream coming out of me swaying around both children, it was like it was being steered towards them through my focus. I was the reason that love could envelop them and penetrate their cells at this moment, and it was bottomless and eternal.

Amazed, I was left standing while this was going on, and I realised that I was experiencing genuine love for the first time in my life. This wasn't something I could think of or create, this living river of love was what I had allowed to enter last night, and which had activated all my cells. This is God, I thought, this is what God is. He had its own consciousness, and He knew everything. My body tingled and pulsed, and it felt like I was immersed in the energy that was pouring from my heart. All day I walked around as if in a cocoon of joy and I couldn't even feel the ground I was stepping on, it was as if I was floating forward with light dancing feet. This continued for several months afterwards. From being full of worry about the future, depressed and with a lousy self-image, to fully knowing that everything was as it should be. I smiled as much as every cell in my body.

After work and dinner were done this new day, I sat down on the couch present within this new being that I had become, I heard a voice inside me telling me to study nursing. It came as a gentle breeze, but the message was unmistakable. Oh no, I thought, that was the last thing that I wanted. My friend was a nurse and we had discussed it a few times. She thought that it must be the perfect profession for me, but I didn't agree. The thought of being part of surgeries or of seeing open wounds made my spine get cold. As a highly sensitive person I didn't like to be close to people who were hurting, I felt their pains as if they were my own, and it drained me quickly. No, the nursing profession was not for me.

As I sat on the couch, I had no doubt that this was the way I was supposed to go, the voice left a certainty that I couldn't shake off. Not only did it tell me what to study, it also left a message about which college I was going to attend. Oh no, not that one, I thought, it was nearby. I had been trying to sell the townhouse we lived in for a long time to get away from my ex-husband. He tried to make life difficult for me, as previously mentioned, and he was not a good father to the kids. My thought was that it would be easier for them to be far away, than to live near someone who wasn't there for them. With the certainty that came in it didn't look like there would be a move over the next few years, at least not far from here. I remembered the certainty I had the night before when I saw the power spread around the neighbourhood, and the voice lingered in my mind: "everything is as it should be, and all is well." Okay, I thought and capitulated, I will apply and see what happens. It was not possible to argue with this power, the all consuming certainty, this is what I had to do.

It was already September so I thought that the deadline to apply would be March/April, starting next autumn. The next day I learned that this school had opened for a new class next January. The deadline was the following week, so I was just in time to apply. The universe had everything under control. Everyone said that it was difficult to get in and that there were always several hundred applications to the forty places that were available. We needed to have top marks in every subject, in addition to extra points to be considered. I didn't understand how this could be arranged even though I had good grades, to get extra points I had to have worked in health care, something I had never even considered. I sent the application thinking that I would just leave everything to God. I couldn't get past the message from Him, and I was raised to obedience. Just in case, I also sent an application to some other schools far away. If I got admitted to one of them then I would have to move, *but* who can change something decided by God Himself? I felt like a naughty little girl who tried her powers, stubborn as a mare. I got admitted to the school I was told I was going to do my studies and I received rejections from the others. Of course, when something is decided at top level it will be so.

Baptised in Fire

After going to bed that night I was left dwelling on the previous night's event. The power of love that came in the night before vibrated strongly, it felt as though the cells were like living organisms. The vision of the stream flowing through everything appeared, and I wondered what happened as it went further out into the cosmos. The questions buzzed around in my head like bees in a hive, but who could answer them? I had never heard of anything like this, and we had neither google nor youtube at the time. I gently sent out a little thought: Jesus, were you participating last night? Something began to tingle around my body. I sent out a stronger thought: Jesus, are you there, and the tingling became more powerful. I sent out the question with more and more force, and each time I felt the tingling getting stronger, so I started saying it out loud and it increased even more. In the end it became so strong I had to sit up in bed with joy rippling and flowing through my whole being. I began to wave my arms and sway my body as I was not able to resist the strong waves of joy, dancing and laughing as the feeling escalated inside.

The tingling and hissing were so intense that I got dizzy as if I was drunk, which made me laugh even more. Thinking that if someone saw me now, they would put me in the psychiatric ward immediately caused another laugh to bubble up, I felt sorry for those who didn't experience the feelings I now had. After a few moments it calmed down and I was able to lie back under the covers while my eyes were as wide as saucers looking up at the ceiling. What was this? There was no doubt that Jesus was present, but what did it mean? Who exactly was Jesus? The only thing that I knew about him were the stories I had been told when I attended the Sunday-school held in our church and at school, it was quite another thing to experience this close contact. Who could I ask, who knew about such experiences? I wanted a physical person who could answer all the questions that were buzzing around in my head. I couldn't sleep for a long time dwelling on the feeling of complete joy and in a state of being totally present in the now. My mind couldn't penetrate the feeling of peace while I slipped into sleep. The sleeping pills which I had needed before were not on my mind, the worries that used to keep me awake didn't exist where I was now.

The time that followed was good, something had fundamentally changed inside. My whole body was constantly tingling and vibrating, and it felt as if I was walking on air for many weeks afterwards. My friend kept asking about the feelings I had after the incident. She told me after the concert that she had felt the energy coming around me, and that she knew it was for me and not for her, so she was excited to hear what had happened. When she heard about my second experience she spontaneously exclaimed; "Oh, you were filled by the Holy Spirit." I had heard about the phenomenon but had no idea what it would mean. She found some verses in the bible in which the disciples described their experiences of being filled with the Holy Spirit, and there it said that the disciples had felt drunk from it. In several places it also said that they were baptised in fire and water which made me sit like a question mark looking at her.

There were many similarities to what I had experienced, and I had certainly felt like I had been drunk when I sat waving my arms and laughing in bed. Would this be possible? Could it really have been the Holy Spirit who came upon me? I couldn't quite believe it, not for little me. What was in the bible happened then, and this couldn't happen in real life, right? How could I find answers? I wondered a lot about the events that had followed each other and prayed every night for help to find answers, but there was silence. After all those powerful experiences in which both physical and visual aspects were involved, the silence now was overwhelming. I had to find the answers and I wanted the truth. The library was my rescue, and I began to scrutinise what I found in esoteric books. No one could tell of similar events, but it was interesting to read philosophical musings from old and new masters. Historical figures such as Socrates and Plato captivated me, and I wondered how they found the wisdom they possessed. My interest in the human mind and development increased, and the Seth material was brought out on a regular basis. There I found many answers to my metaphysical questions, although it did not give me answers to the experiences I had gone through.

A few months after these events, I was at my friend's house for an evening chat. We often met before the children had to go to bed, and we sat in the living room with our coffee cups while the girls were outside playing. After a while she asked gently: "could you try to put your hands on my shoulders and ask if what you feel can be passed onto me?" She wanted to physically feel what I was talking about. The tingling was still vibrating in my body, as if a living anthill had been established in there, and the activity was constant. I replied that we could give it a try, but I could not promise any result. As I said, so I did, I put my hands on her shoulders and prayed that the feelings inside me would be transmitted if possible. The moment I asked, a stream of fire started, it entered the crown chakra, went down my head and neck, through my shoulders and arms, and finally out through both of my hands. This time too, it came in waves, but now the waves consisted of pure fire, they came from above and didn't start below the feet like last time. It burned all the way, and I was left standing glued to the floor, not able to move a muscle until it stopped. While it was going on I got a message: "This is for later in life, it is not for now." It took a long time before it finally gave way.

As I removed my hands from her shoulders, she turned and looked at me with big open eyes: "I am glad you took your hands away, because my spine is on fire." I understood just as little as the last time when the force had come through, and I was completely dumbfounded with surprise. She later told me that she had checked the places where I had held my hands, and she had seen red marks from where I had my hands, they had lasted for days. Once again, I was speechless. Phenomena which no one could explain had turned upside down all my ideas of what was possible, I didn't understand anything. My previous beliefs about the world and what it is, were just a mishmash of questions, the only thing I was sure of was that there was something here that was real and that could not be seen with the mere eyes.

I also knew that God was true, he was alive, I didn't have a shadow of a doubt about that. When the force came the first time it entered with the knowledge of where it had come from: from creation itself, and I also knew that Jesus was involved in some way, but there my thoughts were mixed. The church had in a way taken ownership of him, and there were so many condemnations and dogmas that I couldn't agree with. How could I find the truth? There was no one in my circle of acquaintances who had had similar experiences, and those I tried to talk to about it just looked at me with questions in their eyes. My friend and neighbour was worth her weight in gold, even though she couldn't help me with the answers. She understood as little as I did, but we both loved the discussions about the spiritual and metaphysical world.

The Power of Healing

After these events, I began to lay my hands on friends and acquaintances to see if it had any effect. All of them reported headaches and neck pain that had disappeared, and they all reported that a deep relaxing calm came over them. On a few occasions I received feedback that severe migraine attacks had disappeared, and everyone just wanted to lie down and rest as soon as I took my hands away. All of this piqued my curiosity, and I began to read all I could find about healing. As soon as the opportunity came, and my economy allowed it, I joined weekend courses in meditation and healing.

The first one that I attended was very special. I had heard that a well-known English healer, Matthew Manning, was going to have a workshop in the neighbouring town, and I signed up. It was a powerful experience. In addition to teaching and meditation, he gave us healing while we sat in circles and held hands. He walked around and put his hands on our shoulders, explaining that the energy would flow around to everyone all the time. During healing the second day, we were about thirty people in the group, he started with me. It didn't take long before I felt the woman on my left side starting to lift her right arm in the air. I gently pulled it back down, but it bounced up again at once. Poor girl, I thought, she must have a lot of tension inside. When Matthew finished the round, I suddenly felt his hands on me one more time. The heat spread like fire down my spine and I burst into tears. It happened so fast that I couldn't react with my usual response, to shut down. I sat in the middle of a pile of people who could see me, and I sobbed and cried like a child, it was embarrassing. The desire for the famous hole to come and devour me was huge, but there was nothing to do but let the storm ride out, his healing-powers were stronger than my will.

The next day, the last day of the course, I was still exhausted and wanted to be as anonymous as possible. I sat down in the back row where I rested while listening to what he was conveying. Suddenly I felt a lightning bolt going through me, I recognised him. Four years earlier I had had a dream where I had woken up inside the dream. There I looked towards the end of the bed where I could see a man looking at me. Even though I didn't know him, I wasn't afraid, and there was love throughout the room flooding and vibrating.

In this sphere I awoke totally surprised, thinking that I had already woken up so how could I wake up again? It had felt just as real the first time as the second and I was left feeling disoriented for a while before I could get myself back into the now. As time went by, I forgot the whole episode, but now the memory flooded back like lightning from a clear sky. Was I really meant to meet him? And was it predestined that he would help me with the heavy redemption of the day before? Was this planned? I didn't understand, but I just had to accept what I had experienced, this was yet another mystery I had to figure out. Matthew came back to Norway twice after that before he began his career in research. He went to the United States where they wanted to research cancer cells and how they react to the use of healing.

There wasn't much literature on these topics either in the nineties, but I think that I found most of what was translated into Norwegian. At the time I didn't read English books, so I was dependent on them being in my language. There were many visits to the library, and the blush burned in my cheeks many times over the topics which I presented to the librarian. When I see the big change we have had in the last decades, it is like looking at two different worlds. Today it is natural for almost everybody to talk about healing, meditation, and energy work. We live in a time of rapid change in how we relate to both the seen and unseen worlds, and our understanding of how it works is constantly changing.

I had taken up meditation several years earlier, even if it wasn't easy to find time in a busy life. I tried to practice as often as possible, and I loved to go into myself to get a handle on what could be found there. The experience gave me an insight into the fact that there is something to be found only through going inside. I hadn't been conscious of this before, and I wanted to get to it. The love was very present, but everyday life was busy, and so I had to prioritise, there wasn't enough time to do what I most wanted to do; to reconnect with the experience.

The nursing programme started, and there were a lot of new topics to learn. I enjoyed it from day one and my fellow students were like-minded people where I could be who I am. They ranged in age from early twenties to the fifties, so I was about midway in age. The subjects were so interesting that I devoured the literature we had on the reading list. The more I learned about the human body and how it works, the more fun I found it to be. I also made new friends with whom I spent a lot of time. Life smiled as never before, so it wasn't in my mind that the darkness would show its claws again soon. The joy and unfolding of new learnings at the time was the only existence that could be.

The search for answers continued even during this busy time. Since I knew that God was alive and that Jesus was having a hand in the experience, I started attending some of the meetings with my friend, maybe I could find answers to some of my questions? She was looking for a place to belong, for a community where she could feel at home, I wanted to find the truth. We visited different churches and denominations, and participated in many gatherings that were fine, but there was always something missing. I couldn't feel the unity I had experienced, it was always us and them. Those of us who believed alike could go to heaven, while all the others had to find their way first. The path they were referring to was the one that they saw as right; the others were in perdition which did not resonate with what I had seen and experienced. When God's power poured out of me, everything was covered by love. There was nothing that existed outside, so why was everyone concerned about us and them? Why was it so important to create differences through beliefs? We were all humans trying to live a happy life, weren't we? I couldn't free myself from the fact that there was something that didn't harmonise. I was also told that the books I liked to read came from the devil, and that I had to stay away from anyone who didn't believe in a proper way, so I quietly chose to pull away. My life was so packed with studies, kids, and work, so it went smoothly and without any discussion between my friend and me.

One day during early autumn, two years after the event, I was out in the woods with the kids. We were going to pick lingonberries and they jumped around with berry pickers, eager to find the most. A pleasant late summer heat had returned causing the smell of earth and heather to vibrate in my nose. I took a deep breath as I admired the orange and red colours appearing between the green leaves, autumn was coming, and it was okay. In the past I had dreaded the time when visible signs marked the coming of winter, but not now. My winter depressions were just a vague memory, and I suddenly became conscious of how I was enjoying the richness of the range of colours that I saw around me, it felt like a gift from mother nature. I smiled to myself watching my two healthy, beautiful children running around in delight at every red lingonberry and I felt that my life was complete.

The sun warmed my face as I pulled out one thermos with juice and another with hot sausage and called the children for a break. As soon as they had finished eating, they were running around again having fun, while I went on to clean the berries. It was so good to sit and shake the berry cleaner looking at how the leaves and twigs found their way back to earth, and I felt a special calm arising inside me in this beautiful landscape. The sounds from the children's voices surrounded me as music. I picked away sticks while my thoughts were allowed to flow where they wanted. The question was always there in my mind: why did I have to wait until later? Why couldn't I get the answers now? The love that washed through me had all the answers, so what kept them from coming forward? The experience had given me a boost of joy and positive energy, but I wanted to get to the core, I wanted to understand it all with my mind too. I took in the beautiful surroundings, sniffed the scent of the lingonberries and the smell of birch in a perfect combination with the coffee I poured. It was time to pack up, but first I needed to just feel how good life could be right now and let all questions rest. Two weeks later life was turned upside down once again.

Caught in the Web of Life

The second year had started at the nursing school, and it was time to study psychology. This was something I was really looking forward to. The functionlity of the human mind had fascinated me as far back as I can remember. Already as a twelve-year-old, books about real people had caught my interest, and I loved reading the book series called "The Story of" Florence Nightingale, Madam Curie, Albert Einstein, Mozart, and many others. There were so many who had lived exciting lives, and their courage aroused my admiration. They made choices that went towards their societies' standard and found their own way through listening to themselves. I was already looking forward to becoming an adult and being able to find *my* way. I filled many diaries with dreams and thoughts, wondering how my life would be. In the stories I read, I could empty my thoughts of the strict rules which had been stopping me in my own unfolding. My brother was only one year older than me but was allowed so much more just because he was a boy, so I wished that I had been born as a boy too. Why did it have to be different? It was completely impossible for me to understand, so I just stored this feeling of injustice inside.

Now I wanted to learn more about upbringing and development, and perhaps understand more about how we are affected by the environment in which we grow up. It became far more interesting than I could have predicted. I only had one memory before I was ten years old, the rest was in total darkness, and this memory wasn't something that I wanted to think about as it was painful. I was six years old, and my sister was a newborn. We had a substitute housewife coming daily to help, and this gave my mother room to take trips to the city. One day she asked if I wanted to join her and I felt my heart leap with joy, I was allowed to join my mom for a trip to the city. While I waited for her, I played in the snow outside the house. There had been quite a lot coming the last few days, so it was a pleasure to play in it. When she came out, she scolded me for being full of snow, and I felt guilty for delaying her in the time she could be out. We got most of it brushed off, and we started walking down the street. I jumped and bounced with pure joy at being gifted this adventure alone with my mom. As we walked, I took her hand so that I could feel close to her, but she threw it back and said I was too old to hold hands. I sank into a dark hole and gave myself a promise: I will never let you come near me again and I closed off my heart towards her. I have never been able to remember anything about the trip to the city.

Until I started psychology, I had taken for granted that it was common not to remember our childhood, but now I learned that when someone is repressing years of their existence, something lies behind it. I learned that this is a defence mechanism which sets in when the experience or experiences are too difficult to cope with. It startled me, what was behind the fact that I didn't remember my first ten years? No matter how much I twisted and turned my brain cells, nothing came up. I deliberated and circled around that thought, and looked for books in the library that might help me to find answers. I also asked my parents and siblings to tell me about the time we grew up. All my siblings could talk about one event after another, so why couldn't I? As they recounted it dawned a little, as if a memory deep inside would diffusely materialise.

My mother told me about a time when they were looking for me all afternoon. I was about five years old when it happened. When the evening came and all my friends were about to go to bed, they were worried as I hadn't come home. They knocked on every door, and in the end one of the girls told them she had locked me into an old bomb shelter. I don't remember anything about the incident, but I did remember the place, a cave inside a rock wall near where we lived. During the war they had put in solid iron doors so that people could seek protection when the alarm went off. Inside the cave the darkness was total, no light could enter, and it was damp and raw. Sometimes we played in the area, and we used to peek in with horror-mixed glee. Was that where the repression occurred? At least it provided the answer to a nightmare I had as a child, a dream that popped into my memory when I learned about the incident. I remember the nightmare to this day as if I have just woken up from it.

I am in the basement where we live. There are grey brick walls all around me, and the smell of moisture is sticking to my nose. The wooden door is closed, and a dim light rests in the room. I see myself standing in the middle of the room as a five-year-old girl. Bright curls surround the face which has eyes as big as saucers; they are guarding the door in front, and I am scared. The urge to run upstairs is strong, up where there is light and into the living room where my parents are sitting, but I can't. I am frozen while I sense what is on the other side. I can see three big trolls through the cracks and can see that they follow my every movement. I take a deep breath as I take one step forward. The trolls take a step towards the door too. I take one more step and so do they. Ugh, now they came very close to me, I think, and I back away. Fear makes my little body shiver. How will I get to safety? There is no escape option, I just know it. Suddenly the door is ripped open with a bang, and I jump back. Panic rises when I see a huge black spider in the doorway and the light from the outside streams in between all its legs. If I could just manage to run fast, but I know it will catch me if I try, I cannot escape all its arms. It takes a step into the room, and I reverse back, one gentle step at a time I reverse backwards. Finally, I feel the wall behind me, I can't go any further. I wish someone could come and save me, but I know I must manage myself. I must find a way out. The spider has me in its power and I stand as if nailed to the brick wall.

I remember waking up full of fear and jumping as far from my bed as I could to seek shelter with my mother, the trolls could be hiding under my bed. Right after my mother told the story, the memory came up and I thought that that was where it originated. Many years later the dream reappeared in my memory again when more of the layers were revealed. The fears holding me captive and the feeling that no one could save me, would be answered many, many years later. Right now, I settled on the fact that it showed the fear I had been in during the hours in the bomb shelter as a five-year-old.

The Spider's Net

As I have mentioned, everyday life was full of activities, it was like my brain had changed to become a sponge sucking in new knowledge every day. Blinkers I didn't know were there fell away, giving me new angles to look from and I loved to be in this place of learning. My convictions of right and wrong were reversed, turned around and checked again. I had to agree with myself what was 'out of date', and what I wanted to bring along with me into my new life. My ex-husband kept making trouble for us where he could, he didn't know what cooperation regarding the kids meant. I cleaned an office two afternoons a week, and one weekend per month I worked as a receptionist in a hotel, my economy needed this subsidy so that it would go round. A friendly girl at the public support system helped me put in place how they could support me, for example with things such as school supplies and what resources I needed, to finish my education. What I received for our monthly needs, like food and rent, was minimal. I sometimes asked if their father could pick up our daughter on the after-school programme so that she wouldn't have to go to the cleaning job with me, but he consistently refused, he always replied that I should blame myself as I was the one who had wanted a divorce. Neither of the children enjoyed being with their father and his new family, so this was the only worry at that time.

I clenched my teeth together and did the best that I could. When my son was twelve years old, he talked a lot about not wanting to go to his father every other weekend. He told me about episodes that had been extremely difficult, and he felt his father was not present for him. The three of us met to talk about this, and in that conversation, I discovered how the father turned everything the boy said to his own benefit. I heard how he manipulated his son into feeling sorry for himself, so, I had to stop the father several times and ask if he please could listen to what the boy tried to tell him. It was not possible to turn the father's opinion away from himself, but we eventually agreed that our son could choose the weekends he would go to him. My daughter continued visiting him alone, but often cried and didn't want to go when her father came to pick her up. I thought that if they had been with him during their childhood, they would at least know their origin, as they got older it was better to let them choose for themselves. The responsibility for them knowing both parents lay heavy on my shoulders, and I felt a lot of guilt.

Half of my studies were now finished, and we had been working quite a lot with psychology. As we delved deeper into different topics, I began to ask more questions about why my life was the way it was and what had made me make the choices that I had made? Why did I choose to marry so young instead of getting an education? What made me think that a marriage would save me from the chaos at home? Why did I choose to marry a man with whom I had had several difficulties before we married? Among other things he had demanded to see all my diaries even though he didn't understand the Norwegian language. When I showed them to him, he made a fire out of them and proclaimed that the time before I met him was now gone. It was painful to watch them burn, so why didn't I stop him? Why did I trust his opinions more than mine, and not follow what was right for me? I started questioning everything that had led me to where I was. The teacher talked about the feeling of guilt and how this can deprive us of choice, and I wondered why I felt so much guilt. She also said that this was shaped in the mind during childhood. Since

I didn't have any reference points from my childhood, I couldn't understand where it was coming from. Why was my childhood in the dark? I had to figure this out, but I didn't know how to restore my memories. I had tried to get my family to tell me about my early childhood and I had found old photos, but it didn't lead me to more memories. What other options did I have?

I also dwelled a lot on the momentary change that had occurred after God's love washed through me. How is it possible to experience a complete change in how I perceived the world from one day to the next? Although nothing had shifted on the outside, everything had shifted on the inside. The only times I have experienced anything similar was when the children were born. I remember very clearly standing by the window of the hospital with my first born in my arms, watching people rushing in and out of cars, feeling sorry for them as they just carried on with their normal lives. It was like a new room had opened; "I" had shifted to "us". The world had changed into a place where only love and peace existed. When I felt the presence of the little baby in my arms, I came into a feeling of richness I had never experienced before. All the people I saw out there were occupied with their everyday lives whilst on their way to activities or work, but for me there was nothing to do. Everything was perfect. The tiny life I held in my arms was the only important thing for me now.

Looking back at this memory today, I understand that this new little life had brought with it a revelation of truth. This truth became pushed into the background as everyday life kept me busy with a lot of doing and all the external activities took over. No one tells us that inner experiences are just as important as external ones, that is something we must figure out for ourselves if we want to go down that path. As it was at the time, I began to ask even more questions and I had to find the answers. My parents' constant disagreements were something I had always lived with, and I understood that they had somehow shaped my way of perceiving the world I was living in. The rules of right and wrong were rigid and not something to even question. Every time I argued about what was said, there were beatings and punishments, so I learned early in my life to be quiet, the less I said the safer the surroundings.

It began to dawn on me how these frames had coloured my view of the world as an unsafe and dangerous place. Since the world was scary, I needed to find a new frame in which to exist. From such a point of view, even marriage seemed to be the safest place to live, the big world was too unsafe and scary for me to dare move around in it alone. Marriage became equally filled with rigid rules, as was natural since I would automatically choose the familiar. I didn't understand this at the time, but now I can look at it with completely different eyes and understanding; like attracts like. As life felt more and more narrow, he would always choose who my friends were and how I could dress, it felt like I wore a noose around my neck. Slowly it tightened until I could no longer breathe. That was when all the pain occurred in my body, and I was diagnosed with fibromyalgia. I was also not allowed to get an education, which I began to miss more and more. Although it was a tough process, I eventually managed to break out. The pain eased considerably, and I started the study skills I needed to be able to move on. Now I was about to finish nursing.

Since I wanted to know the reason behind my suppression of my childhood, I read a lot of literature on various topics. In addition, I asked to be guided to where I needed to go to find out more of what I didn't know. One night I had a dream that was stronger than any dream I had had in a long time. The feelings were so real I couldn't shake them off afterwards.

I run as fast as my small feet can. The darkness is dense, and I am so scared that it is difficult to breathe. The frozen ground sends small needles of shivers up through the soles of my feet, but I hardly notice them. The trees and the bushes are growing close to the path and branches are grabbing my nightgown as if they want to hold me back, but nothing can stop me. I glimpse an opening further ahead and pray that there is someone there to save me. The taste of blood in my mouth is strong and I am tired, I just want to lie down and be swallowed up by the ground, but I can't, someone is coming after me and it is dark and dangerous. I must find a place to hide. The sound from a branch cracking sends chills down my spine, 'help me', a silent scream vibrates out, but not a sound comes from my lips. Then I notice the outline of a house and breathe a sigh of relief. There is probably someone there who can save me, I think, and I fly up the stairs and through the door. The hallway I enter is dimly lit and I can tell that the house is empty. I feel the emptiness like a punch in my stomach, there is no one there! The stairs up to the next level of the house are right in front of me and I take my flight up. I can see rows of doors on both sides, but I chose the one at the end of the corridor, the one furthest away from the stairs. There I jump into the bed placed alongside the wall and pull the covers firmly over my head. The only thing I hear is the sound of the fuse box humming. My heart is pumping like crazy, and it is difficult to breathe. I try breathing slowly to silence my heart while listening to footsteps. Now I can hear that someone is on their way up, and I almost stop breathing for fear of being discovered.

I woke up with a jerk and gasped for air as if I was holding my breath, I felt my heart thump like crazy. What was this? The dream had felt so real that I needed time to recover. The horror lingered in me for a long time, as if an old fear had been brought back to life. There was something familiar about it, as a recollection which I couldn't quite get my hands on. The little girl who ran for her life, what did she run from? The sound of the fuse box thundering was a familiar phenomenon, it made me think of the summer holidays with my grandparents and I remembered now I used to lie in bed and listen for footsteps. Did the dream show me something I needed to remember? I squeezed my brain for days but got nowhere. In one of the books I had read during the study of psychology, there were some descriptions of signs of abuse. When I read these, I stopped several times, and I wondered about all the things I recognised in myself. Many of these symptoms don't have to stem from abuse, but why did so many equal my own way of thinking? Could there be blocked incidents stemming from such a thing? If so, who could it be? I was pretty sure it couldn't be my own father; I could use a lot of nouns on him that weren't pretty, but something like this I was sure couldn't come from him.

The dream made me intensify my search for the truth about my childhood, so I eventually decided to try hypnosis. I had read that this could help to bring back memories, so I thought that it might be worth a try. I also wanted to be sure that they knew their subject, it had to be someone with good references. No one I knew of had done this, so it felt like I was looking for a needle in a haystack. I asked God and my guides to help me find someone if this was a good way to find an answer. After my experience I had a completely different relationship with the invisible, now the contact felt close and natural, something I had never been conscious of before. Asking for help when I was stuck had helped me many times in the past, but now I did it with a trust that I hadn't felt before. I tried again.

A Window Through Hypnosis

Shortly after I decided to find a hypnotherapist, I went to visit a friend of mine. We crawled onto her couch, one of us at each end, and we started talking about everything and nothing. I held the coffee mug and sniffed the good scent as we shared the latest events in our lives. She was just as alternative in her thinking as I was, so it was good to air our thoughts and opinions. Here I could say everything bluntly and I got a lot of good reflections back. She told me that she was expecting a group from India who was coming to Norway soon, and they were going to travel around to different places to give healing. The group was made up of three people who used to travel around Europe, helping people to become free from both physical and mental difficulties. I listened carefully as I felt something was activated inside me. I asked if they used hypnosis, to which she replied in the affirmative. I booked an appointment there and then, it felt like the universe had heard my prayers and had put the answer right in my hands. Joy and gratitude rippled through me as I walked home afterwards, the feeling of being seen and guided was strong, maybe I wasn't so alone in everything after all? Even if I felt the closeness of those around me, I was surprised every time they responded so quickly. I had a lot of responsibilities; being a single mum with two kids, studying and working on the side, so I often found myself alone with all I had to do and take care of. Now I felt the answers to my prayers for help and I felt totally supported. This strengthened my belief that my guides were there, and that they saw me and heard me.

The day of the appointment dawned, and I went with a feeling that fate had set this in motion. It was a warm day in early September, the sun was shining, and I could hear the birds chirping through the open car window. The breeze felt warm as if summer was still lingering in the air. How I love this extension of warmth that brings out the scents of the earth. I inhaled deeply while the feeling of excitement and scarcity rushed through my body, both at the same time. What would come to light? Would anything come up, or was it a dead end? I just had to be open and let everything develop by itself, the way this group suddenly showed up after I decided to try hypnosis was a sign for me this was a good choice. When the universe put this in my path I wanted to respond with confidence.

The woman who was going to do the session was mature, and I felt immediately that she was trustworthy. She had an aura of gentleness and motherly love that made me relax, and her eyes greeted me directly as if she saw more than just me. The room was filled with a lovely scent, and I could see the incense lit on a table and the smoke swirling around in the room. The curtains were drawn so that the sunlight would not disturb, and candles were lit and put in several places. The bench was ready and looked soft and comfortable, she gave a sign for me to go lie down and came with a blanket which she pulled over me with a smile. I felt a calmness seep in through the atmosphere and this great woman's presence, it was as if my senses perceived something my mind could not see, and this something instilled peace and trust. I settled down and took a deep breath.

In the beginning she spent time getting me into the state that signifies hypnosis. My belief had been that consciousness needed to be completely gone, but what I experienced was a totally relaxed presence, where images appeared out of nowhere, she asked questions and pictures came out by themselves. On one occasion I saw the room that I used to have when I was on vacation at my grandparents'. I saw it from the outside and the window stood out with a darkness that brought out a strong resistance, so I didn't say anything, I didn't want to go there. She still managed to get me to understand what had happened without me having to see it. One question after another got me into the story that unfolded and finally, I burst into tears. I told her that my grandfather had molested me, with the voice of a little girl. Part of me registered it with amazement, while the feeling of wanting to crouch down into the foetal position and disappear, was strong. She eventually asked me if I wanted to talk to him, if I had any questions I wanted to ask, and I said yes. The first thing coming out of me was why. He replied that he couldn't help it, he was just so fond of little girls. When we finished speaking, she helped me through a very strong process of forgiveness and when that was completed, I felt peace.

Back in the car I felt completely empty looking up into the sky, was it possible that this had happened to me when I was a little girl? The age that had emerged during the session was five years old, that's when it had started. I knew that nothing had happened after I was ten, so that had to be the time that the abuse had stopped. Is this what made me shut down my memories? I decided to seek out a cousin and tell her about this surprising discovery. The thoughts jumbled around, and I didn't know if I could trust what had been shown to me. She will probably be totally shocked when I tell her all this about our grandfather, I thought. It wasn't a long drive to her house so ten minutes later I drove into the road where she lived, parked the car, and rang the doorbell. Luckily, she was home alone, and we walked in while we were chatting. The coffee was put on the table, and she looked at me with a searching gaze as we sat down in the living room.

She could see that I was thinking about something, and I was dreading telling her. How to convey such a message in a gentle way? It wasn't possible so I just burst out with all I had discovered that day. The reaction wasn't quite as I expected, to say the least, she looked at me and said she wasn't surprised. I glanced at her with an open mouth taken by surprise. "What do you mean?" I asked. "He did the same to me, she answered, "he abused many that I know of, so the fact that you also did experience this doesn't surprise me". I just looked at her with an open mouth, totally surprised. "What on earth are you saying?" I replied, "how could this go on around me without me having any clue, not a single suspicion? How can anything like this be kept so concealed?" She shrugged and said that no one had been allowed to say anything, then she begun to talk while I listened in total surprise, unable to comprehend that this had been around me without my having had any inkling of it. She told me that she had approached him when she was fourteen years old to ask him why he did it. When she told me his answer I surrendered to this truth, and I told her that it was the exact same words he had said to me in the hypnosis session.

I was shaken to my core, at the same time feeling that many pieces had fallen into place. My conviction that men just wanted my body and weren't really interested in me, my scepticism and distrust, it all fitted in. My feeling of being different, of being the black sheep in the family may also have originated from there. It was as if I understood myself in a way in which I had never done before. Although I was in shock, I also felt a kind of peace, I knew that it was necessary to shed light on what my memory had kept away from me. This story had to come to light, and it was a tough message. The surprise could not have been greater, but now it was possible to process. If it had stayed hidden, I could have done nothing to heal my wounds, there it would go on living its own life and control my thoughts and reactions. I knew this to be true. Now I could finally get behind the reasons for my many automatic reactions and beliefs. After we finished talking, I went to my parents' home to share what I had discovered, I needed to know if they knew what had been going on in the family.

We were in the kitchen the three of us, my parents and I, it was now late afternoon. My mother was busy cleaning up after dinner while my father sat by the kitchen table. I was too nervous to sit down so I just leant against a chest of drawers, to have some support for my shaky legs. Where would I start? Feelings weren't something we had ever talked about or expressed, and now I had to delve into the darkest area in our family. I had learned early on to keep things to myself, this was the toughest I had experienced so far. Many times, when I had cried as a child, my father had told me to stop. He used to say that if I didn't stop right away, he would give me something to cry for. The beating we received from him was not with a gentle hand, so I soon learned to swallow my tears and to be quiet.

I took a deep breath and began whilst my whole body was shivering inside. This wasn't something I wanted to convey, but I had to. I didn't say many sentences before my father got up and rushed out, it happened so suddenly it felt as if he was running intuitively. Did he know what I was about to tell? I let him disappear while I told my mother everything. She just stood quietly looking at me as I talked, and afterwards she exclaimed that she had never liked him. There had been something about him she had felt was not good, so because of that she had taken extra care of my younger sister when we were on the island where my father's family lived. I just looked at her and realised that she was never going to be any support and help.

I left with a sadness for all the feelings which they couldn't admit were there. I understood how limited and painful it must have been to live a life where emotions could never be expressed, the facade was so important that they had stopped themselves from living. The fact that she had looked after my sister and not me, was okay. My older brother and I had always gone to the island with our father, while my mother and sister stayed behind with my grandmother. They would come sometime later. I didn't like it at my grandmother's, so if they had refused to let me go, it would have been even worse. With my father's family there was always a lot of laughter and fun, there were many families living around, aunts and uncles and a lot of cousins to play with. We went fishing using rowing boats, made fun of whatever we could find in nature, explored the island, always creative and full of laughter. It was two months with play and freedom, unity, and storytelling. Perhaps the unity was so strong because of the dark secret lurking in the corners of the room? Although it was now out in the open, I felt great gratitude for the holidays with my family, I would not have wanted to be without these times. Of course, I would rather be without the secret lurcking in the corners, like a snake crawling around hidden in the grass, but the holiday's fun was more important than anything. I also felt loved and cared for by my grandmother and other family members in a way I had never felt at home.

I heard a voice which came into my mind as I headed home; "everything is as it should be." A room which until then had been closed and locked was now open for the light to shine in. A dream I had many years ago appeared in my mind.

I am standing in something resembling a big hall where there are three doors. They look the same, all made of solid wood with iron fittings. The door handles are made of wrought iron, and it looks like they haven't been opened for a long time. I know I am inside my heart, and I am looking around the room where a dim red light brightens up the space so that I can see where I am going. One of the doors draws me in, but as I approach it a fierce fear grows inside me. The closer I get the greater the fear becomes. I know that the other doors are not dangerous, but this one is, so I am not going to open the one attracting me. I just know that if I go in there I will never come back. This door is forbidden.

Was this the door which I had just opened, I wondered, as I recalled the feeling of disaster I had when I woke up. It was a lot to take in, and I slowly drove home. My feelings were in a turbulent mix of surprise, disbelief, anger, confusion, and acceptance. I knew that what had been revealed during the day was true, what I couldn't fathom was how this could have played out without my having had a hint of suspicion. I knew that this secret had to be revealed, I couldn't heal before it was in the open. Perhaps many of my difficulties could have been avoided if I had known earlier?

When that thought entered, a fierce hatred suddenly flew up from somewhere deep inside me. It wasn't aimed at anyone; it just came as if a monster had been let out of its hiding place. A naked flame rose from the depths, and the force quickly absorbed everything it encountered. I felt how easy it was to let it take up residence. The thought of what an adult could do to a small innocent child would justify the existence of that hatred. I could taste it, it had a bitter-sweet taste that was captivating, and I felt the flame take over my whole being. It was so intense that I immediately understood; if I let it take over, then there would be no room for love. I also knew that it was up to me to choose sides: hate or love?

Thoughts of my dad's rage, the beatings and punishments, my husband's control over me, and now this. All significant men in my life that could justify the hate, and me being deprived from the memories from my whole childhood, but I knew I had a choice. The inner knowing I received while God's love washed through me, that everything is as it should be, came back to me. Okay, I thought, I choose love. I saw and felt how easily I could have chosen to hate. It was as if I could see how that what I had experienced had coloured my entire existence and how the secrecy had contributed to my not being able to process it, to heal. A saying that I had heard a lot through the years growing up, "you are not hurt by what you don't know," came into my mind, and I laughed out loud. What nonsense, I thought, what I now knew had to come to light to heal and to be free. What I don't know, what is in my shadow, I thought further, will in the end destroy me. The power lying there is constrained, like the hatred that suddenly appeared. I had no idea that there was such a thing in my energy field, but it felt old. Maybe older than me?

I calmly drove home, parked the car, and walked in. The house was empty as the children were being taken care of by their friend's families, it gave me some time to gather myself after the events of the day. When I chose love, the hatred had melted away. It had felt like a tornado of force running down my entire body, leaving silence inside as it slipped out. I was exhausted, but at the same time I felt calm and grateful. What I had been made aware of was so strong it was almost impossible to fathom. Had hatred taken over, love would not have been able to live inside me, they couldn't exist in the same environment. If love was absent, I couldn't pass the most important thing on to my children, or anyone else for that matter. After my experience of God's love, there was nothing that could measure up to it. I wanted to go back to that at whatever cost, even the feeling of justice the hatred had brought in, was less important.

If I had had the possibility, I would have taken a leave of absence from my studies, but it was out of the question. I would have lost the economic help I had been receiving from the social department, and I needed to have an education to be able to sustain our family life. The feeling I had was equal to the feeling in my dream where the spider was hindering my escape from the damp, dark cellar, I was trapped and couldn't get out. It was difficult to do my internship period, study for the exams and complete all the assignments that needed to be done, while at the same time wanting to get to the bottom of everything that had come to light. "As this present day, your strength shall be." The sentence appeared every morning before my mind woke up and before my reality was in place. It was like living in separate rooms, one at work and one at home with the kids. The words helped me to stay focused on where I was at the moment. When I collapsed into bed at night, I gave thanks to God that everything had gone well, we had managed this day too.

Family Secrets Revealed

It is almost funny how we manage to adapt when we must. I found a rhythm that worked, so I was able to finish my education in the end. As I stood with the diploma in my hand, I felt the tears press behind my eyes, the fact I had managed was a great victory. Now I could call myself a nurse, and could start a life without books that needed to be read or assignments to be handed in. I had already got a job in homecare, and I was looking forward to starting. Finally, I could lower my shoulders and maybe make time for my own needs. I began to understand the voice that told me the experience was for later in life. Everything had to happen in the right order, nor would I have been able to squeeze in anything but studies, work, and children.

Fortunately, the kids did well, and they had a lot of friends who often visited us. Although our economy was tight, they were creative and kept coming up with something fun to do. One summer they came home carrying planks they had found thrown down in the woods nearby and began to make a cabin out on the terrace. I had to laugh when I discovered what they were doing, and they managed to make a little cabin all by themselves. Since I occasionally had to work in the evening, I had found a nanny whom they became very fond of. She began to take my daughter to the stables, and it was love at first sight. She learned to ride and how to take care of the horses, and as she got older, we arranged it so that she could have the responsibility for a horse a few days a week. My son also had good friends, so now

I could relax and spend some long-awaited time alone. The work suited me perfectly, and there was a lot of humour and laughter in the office as we always started with some juicy jokes before we went to work on our duties. None of the days were alike, and the contact with the people I visited was great. I loved to meet people in their homes and not as a nurse in a white uniform running from one hospital bed to the next. When I started in homecare, we had time to talk to the people we visited, and I got to hear a lot of stories that deeply affected me.

Although my parents lived nearby, they didn't help much. When I asked, they looked after the children occasionally, but otherwise we lived our separate lives. They never asked me how things were going or anything about what I had told them. I accepted that they couldn't deal with what had come out, so I was grateful to have my cousin close by. We talked a lot and went on walks in the woods with the kids or to a cabin on weekends, our sons were the same age and they loved playing together. It was a good time, safe and comfortable. I had no need to meet men, although we occasionally went out to dance and shake the everyday responsibilities away. We were equally fond of dancing and music and had many fun experiences which we chatted and laughed about for a long time after.

Twelve years passed before someone showed up who wouldn't let go. For three months he called every week and invited me out and each time I came up with an excuse to decline, but in the end, I gave in and said yes to a meeting. He was a warm and friendly man to talk to, he listened and gave good feedback, and he gave me a feeling of being seen in a good way. The conversations flowed easily, and I found many of the subjects we discussed interesting, so I started to talk to him regularly. One of the things I noticed was his care which was a new experience, and, in the beginning, I was sceptical and wondered how long it would last.

I will never forget the day I capitulated. I was visiting friends in their caravan where they always had their vacation, and the summer was at its best. My friend and I sat chatting on the deck outside the caravan with our coffee cups between us, while enjoying the view of the fjord. The sun sparkled in the water and the scent of coffee mingled with the scent of the salty sea and pine trees, the sky was cloudless and clear, blue as only a summer's day can be. It was a moment of presence, of peace and harmony, as we sat and talked about life. A lovely holiday feeling was getting under my skin, and I felt my shoulders slump. In this good atmosphere I decided to tell her about the new man I had met a few times who would not leave me alone. After a couple of minutes, she said he sounded rare, and asked why I was so sceptical, then she asked me to call him up and ask if he wanted to come and visit us, she wanted to have a look at him, to see if he could be the man for me. I did as she said, I called, and he said yes right away.

After a couple of hours he arrived, and I was wondering how this would go, I felt fear lurking around in my body. After a little chat we went down to the water to have a swim in the sea. I had always been a little anxious about walking into seaweed and sat on the edge of the pier to gather the courage to go into the water. As I sat there, I saw him start to pull up the seaweed waving in the water's crust. I didn't say anything, just observed his eager activity while my friend and I continued talking. When he came back to where we were sitting, he said everything was ready to enter the sea, I could go into the water without fear of any crabs biting my toes. We went down to the water and there I saw a path of sand shining between the seaweed waving in the water. I felt tears in my eyes from this unexpected gesture of kindness, no one had ever done something like this for me. The care I felt emanating from him came from a great heart, and a man with such a heart I could trust and surrender to. I was captivated and there was no turning back.

We started spending every weekend together. My son had just moved to his own place, but he came on an occasional visit. We went on boat trips, spent the night in the boat on one of the islands in the archipelago or had barbecues in his garden. There were social gatherings where friends were invited or just us and all the children. He had a son and a daughter, the same as I, so it was a lot of playing and laughter when we gathered. It felt as if life was filled with life, something I had wanted my children to experience for years. Finally, I felt life smiling at me, I was living my deepest dreams. After one year of travelling between his and my home we moved in together and everyday life continued with a lot of life. We had plenty of room, so both of his children moved in permanently. Friends went in and out, and at times they more or less moved in with us. I used to count the pairs of shoes in the hallway to see how many people were inside when I woke up in the morning, or when we came home from a dinner with friends. Sitting in the kitchen was like sitting next to the highway at times, young people passing in and out. We added more space to the house to create rooms for all our kids and made a small department just for the two of us, the kitchen became the heart of the house, a place everyone sought to go. Eventually my son moved in too.

It was good to have all of the children under the same roof. This was what I had always dreamed of: a family that could enjoy themselves together and share everyday life and fun. When I escaped into marriage the first time, I had hoped that it would be as it was now, but in such an extended family there would undeniably be a lot of drama. Sometimes I could exclaim; "Hotel Cæsar" (a Norwegian drama series) "is nothing compared to this." During this time my daughter had a son, and since she was a single mum, she really appreciated our assistance. He was loved from day one. After he was born the baby's father wanted to contribute, so when the baby was old enough, they arranged for him to be with his father every other week. The little sunbeam, as I called him, had a solid family caring for him on both sides, and the young parents were grateful and happy for the support they received.

There were often family dinners at our place where families from both sides gathered. My mother was often sick, but she came with the breathing machine in tow and my father as her right hand and assisted whenever she needed help. He was the one making dinner and cleaning their house, they therefore greatly appreciated the gatherings at our home, and I was happy to be able to contribute to the family's unity. There was always a loving atmosphere when we were together, but there was still no openness. Every time I tried to get her to talk about her upbringing I was met with silence and her saying there was nothing to tell, and the distance she surrounded herself with did not lend itself to confidential conversations. The day she died I got the call from my sister, and I could tell she was in shock, she just told me to come right away.

I dropped everything I was doing and drove forty-five minutes in no time. The paramedics were standing outside when I arrived, and they asked if I was the doctor. They had tried resuscitation without result and were now waiting for the doctor to write the death certificate before they left. The fact that they took me to be the doctor says something about how calm I was. My mother was still lying on the floor in her bedroom when I entered, and I stopped in the doorway looking at her and hoped she was in a better place now. There was no mourning, just sadness about the life she had lived, it was as if she had never dared to live as her fear of being true to herself had taken away her joy and love. The art she dug herself into became her world, she painted many beautiful pictures on rocks and reefs, and made a lot of tapestries and patchwork until her body couldn't take it anymore. Now she lay like a stranger on the floor, someone I had never been allowed to know. There were no accusations or anger, just a great sadness she had not dared to unfold, now it was too late to change anything, too late to get to know her. Who was she now when her body wasn't her home anymore, I wondered, as I walked into the living room. My father and sister were sitting in silence. They had done everything they could to revive her and now there was nothing more to do.

After my mother was gone, my father gained greater freedom as he no longer needed to be at home to nurse his wife and could travel whenever he wanted. He went on a couple of trips to the south with me and my husband, and some trips to his childhood home after several years of not visiting the place. The siblings who were still alive greatly appreciated his visits, they had been a large family, and several had died through the years he couldn't visit. On one of the trips one of my brothers joined him. While waiting for the flight home they stopped at one of my father's sisters to have a chat. There they started to talk about their childhood and my aunt told them about her experience as a child. My father came home in shock, he said he had never been aware of what was going on behind his back. His sister had said that they had tried to protect him from the suffering that was part of his sisters life, and nothing was said in the years that followed. We had a good conversation and I explained to him that even though he didn't know anything, he probably felt there was a lot left unsaid, a small child knows when those who are around are not doing well. This something can then be left as a feeling for which there are no words. No wonder he had a violent anger that could explode out of nothing. For the first time we could talk about these things without him being defensive. My brother was very relieved that he no longer had to choose who to believe, me, or my father denying what I said.

My husband brought it up one day when we had a quiet moment on the terrace alone. The coffee cups were on the table between us, and we enjoyed the beautiful view of the fjord. Traffic of boats going in and out of the city had slowed down, but there were still many people rushing in and out. A woodpecker was eagerly occupied in the pine tree at the far end of the ornament, and the sound of its rhythmic chopping accompanied the chirping of the birds while they ate from the food my husband always provided for them. "I am so happy you are finally getting justice from your family," he suddenly exclaimed. I looked surprised at him; "life isn't fair," I replied, "it is just a concept we use to judge someone or something, but I am very glad my brother no longer has to choose who to believe." It was one of those moments of clarity.

When my husband made the comment, I instantaneously knew my mission was to be honest, how they reacted was secondary. Everything was as it should be, my siblings had their stories and challenges, I had mine. It was so clear to me as we sat and talked, and I could easily understand how the principle of justice contributed to conflicts in families. "If we could understand that life is as it is," I continued, "if we can put aside the demands which allow us to fight each other, there would be peace." It was like I was staring into eternity and the filter was gone, when we don't have peace with ourselves, we can't create peace on the outside. I was grateful that the truth had finally come out, maybe it could contribute to more openness in my family? We continued the conversation about how expectations over what is perceived as fair, especially during inheritance, tear family members apart. In my mother's family too, there was a split in that regard. I sent up a quiet prayer of gratitude for yet another valuable insight.

My life continued with further education in psychiatry and a busy family life. There was no one in my circle who was thinking about spiritual questions, so I held these thoughts to myself. Every time I tried to bring deeper topics into the conversation or talk about what happened to me, I only got strange looks and the conversation quickly turned to other topics. I still wanted to find the truth of what had happened to me, and I couldn't find it anywhere. My heart cried out many times: when will the time come? If I had known where I could find help I would have rushed to that place, but I had no idea where to look. I missed connecting with like-minded people, people who knew what I was talking about and allowed me to vent the thoughts and ideas which I found interesting. I had found a couple of friends who were on my vibe, allowing me to be more authentic, but there was no time to nurture these new friendships, there was always something else calling me: mutual friends who invited us to dinner, golf tournaments, and trips my husband wanted us to take. Although it was a lot of fun, I felt something beginning to move inside me, an uneasiness that had been there for a long time intensified and became clearer. In all things social there was a longing that was not satisfied, and I felt something began to pull inside me more and more, the experience of 1991 when God's love washed through me, started to rise more consciously in my mind. The feeling of being different also started to creep in again after many years of not being present.

Sometimes I tried to talk to my husband about the thoughts and needs I felt, but he didn't understand what I was referring to. In retrospect I know that what I was chasing was an experience, an inner feeling, and as soon as the words came into play it all came out wrong. No matter how much I tried to talk about it or explain, the words were always left behind in the back of what I wanted to say. How to make others understand what I was unable to grasp? One who has not had such an experience themselves could not know what I was talking about except as a theoretical concept. I felt the time approaching when this was supposed to be addressed and I wanted to start now, but where and how? My patience was really tested.

The Magical Power of Fragrance

From an outside view we lived an enviable life with travels around the world, a large social circle, and everything else we needed. After many years where vacations were just a dream, I now lived with confidence at every point. The love was strong, but there were some areas where I felt great pain and I tried to address what was on my mind many times without my husband being able to meet what I tried to convey. The openness I had met in the beginning suddenly stopped after we got married. I knew he loved me, so how could he shut down so immediately? A wall had built up over the last years and I had no idea how to tear it down. The thought of breaking up another marriage weighed heavily on me, would I have to go through that process again? What would my life be like if I did? Would I make it financially? I had a solid education so it would certainly go smoothly, but I was no longer young, and hadn't worked in the public sector for many years, would I still be attractive as an employee? Could I continue the life we lived and at the same time search for the truth I had to find?

There were so many thoughts I had to keep to myself, and every time I tried to share them with my husband I was rejected. Family life had always been important to both of us, and we had created many bonds through the years. This made it extra difficult to break out and

I strongly wanted it to work out between us so that I could avoid the pain of tearing up these bonds. I began to find myself alone in my world again, a feeling I had felt from time to time throughout my life. We had similar values that brought us together, now I felt my need to find answers to all the questions, which I had, drawing me inwards, while life with him was pulling me outwards. I weighed the pros and cons, what should I do?

Time passed and a growing frustration was building up inside me. I wanted to continue my family life, but at the same time I wanted to put an end to the growing inner pain. The thought of being alone again was terrifying, as a mature adult in my fifties should I start all over again? Was it possible to bridge the distance that had emerged in the last few years? The decision was taken on one of our trips, and it came all by itself. We were in the Dominican Republic with a group of friends. The surroundings were magical, the most romantic place one could think of. A pleasant round of golf was finishing on a golf course that looked like it had been taken out of a travel magazine. The irreducible grass contrasted beautifully with white sandy beaches running along the fairways, and the bunkers (small or big holes filled with sand in which the golf ball can be caught) shone like white eyes between all the green fields. The sea sparkled and became alive in the sunbeams dancing on the water from the golden sun shining above. On the horizon I could see the sea and sky in total reunion, it was not possible to see where one ended and the other started. The temperature was perfect, warm, but with a breeze cooling the skin, it was one of those days where I had to pinch myself on the arm over all the beauty mother nature showed me. The breeze brought with it floral scents from all the plants surrounding the course, they were almost mesmerising in their powers. It was a pleasant round with lots of laughter and togetherness and we completed the whole experience with a great lunch before we went our separate ways.

When we entered the suite, I went out onto the terrace and sat down. There was a beautiful view out to the sea, and I could admire large coconut palms swaying in the breeze along a white beach. My husband went to bed to rest until dinner, this was a regular ritual, while I sat quietly admiring the beautiful picture in front of me thinking this must be the best place to be for couples in love. A strong loneliness came in as I thought about how it could have been, here I was with a man I loved very much, but with a deep loneliness inside me. Why did it have to be like this? Was what I sought impossible to find? Was I demanding too much? The only thing I understood as I sat contemplating, was that this couldn't continue the way it was, I had to take the feeling inside me seriously.

It was like a clarity opened and I realised that I had to leave this marriage as well. I thought about the life we had lived together, all the times we had been on trips, and I just wanted to run home and pack my things. What had led us to this situation? How come I allowed this to be this way? I couldn't change his mind and behaviour, the only thing I was responsible for was my own actions and how I wanted my life to be. The warm breeze sweetened my skin and the scents of exotic flowers vibrated around me, it was as if nature was opening my pores and giving me the answers that I was searching for. It felt as if the vibrations from the fragrances lifted me up to understand what I had to do. I knew now, the certainty hung heavy in the air, but there was also a sense of relief in knowing what was right for me to do.

After the inner struggle of making the decision was over, I felt a new sense of calm. My previous expectation of something I wanted from my husband was gone and it made the rest of the vacation easier. I had decided not to say anything until we were back home so that the holiday could remain without inner turmoil and discussions. The previous times I had wanted to go home and pack my stuff, he had always managed to persuade me to stay. This time was different. The decision was taken with clarity and with an inner calmness, and it was to be done correctly. For the rest of the holiday, I decided to enjoy the surroundings of the most remote place I had ever visited and sucked in all the impressions to use the energy in the time ahead.

Sometime after we got home, I had the opportunity to have a conversation with my husband. The children and grandson kept stopping by daily even though they had their own homes, and I wanted to find a time when I was sure we weren't disturbed. He wasn't surprised that I wanted to leave, but he thought the timing could have been better. There were some events in the family in proximity, so he asked if we could wait to announce the split until it was over. We agreed to wait, and life continued as before, and a part of me breathed a sigh of relief that I didn't have to start the moving process right away. It wasn't easy to break the bonds we had built up, and I know many people give up on their own process to avoid this phase, which I do understand. The fear of the unknown lurked in the nooks and crannies, but it couldn't take over the clarity I had received, this was something I had to go through.

Time went by and life continued as it had been for many years. Sometimes it felt like I was standing in quicksand, and it held me tight like a vise. I tried to untangle myself, but I just felt the grip getting tighter. After a couple of years, I knew I had to act on the decision. We both knew that the marriage was over so why wait? He knew that the battle was lost and we were finally able to tell family and friends about it. It was good to let the cat out of the bag and be open instead of holding it inside, and the relief I felt that the wait was over was good feedback that the decision I had made was correct.

There were loud protests from a part of my family when I told them about the split, they couldn't understand why we had to make such a drastic change as we were good friends, while others understood and had seen it coming for some years. I felt the security that had been my everyday life for a long time was now disappearing, I had to take care of myself. The traditions around the holidays and family events would also change. How would the celebrations look now? The future lay in an uncertain mist in front of me and it was scary, I didn't know anything anymore and what I was moving into was brand new. When I got divorced the first time it was necessary to be able to survive, if I had stayed, I would have become sick. As previously mentioned, I was diagnosed with fibromyalgia and the pain only increased over the last years I was married. This time I had a good life in so many ways and family life was tough to lose, unity and security were important to both of us and now I was about to tear it apart again. My conscience gnawed, but I knew that there was no turning back, should I ever have time for myself and what I had to figure out I could no longer compromise. When one door closes, a new one opens, it is incredibly fascinating to see in retrospect how the universe plays the cards. What followed next I couldn't even have dreamed of. It was as if this had been waiting for me outside the comfort zone I was in, and as long as I stayed there nothing would have changed. I had to make up my mind and go through some fears before new adventures could come into my life.

A Visit from the Other Side

I felt in every cell in my body that something new was about to unfold. What this 'new' would be I had no idea, I just felt something in the air. For the first time ever, I was going to live all by myself and the first thing I had to do was to find a place to live. My husband agreed to come with me to look at houses which I was very grateful for, he was detail oriented while I saw the whole picture. I wanted to find something that *felt* right, so it was good to have someone who could see with a critical eye. It only took a few days before I had found a small house that looked very interesting, and we went to have a look at it. As soon as I walked in, I felt that this was my home, it was perfectly located close to the city, but in a quiet area at the end of a cul-de-sac. The view was beautiful, and the sun was shining in from large windows when we entered. The garden was like a small dream where the owner had created an oasis of rose bushes and small trees. There was no lawn to be maintained, only slabs laid between the stone beds where rose bushes were standing in full bloom. In the back of the tiny garden there was a small space with walls and a roof. They had made an outdoor fireplace and clusters of grapes were hanging from the ceiling, I could clearly picture family and friends gathering around the table having a nice dinner, or myself with a notebook and a cup of coffee. This beautiful oasis invited both coziness and creativity so fortunately we both agreed that it was a perfect place for me.

The bidding that went on the next day was so exciting that I got stomachache. We were both sitting out on the patio, and I waltzed in and out while drinking one cup of coffee after another. The time went slowly forward minute by minute every time I made a new bid, would the other party give up now? I just *had* to have it, and my husband was just as intent on winning the bidding round as I was on living in the house. After a few rounds, the message I had been waiting for finally came, the house was mine. Tears of joy and relief welled up as if my body had a hard time containing so much delight. I waited impatiently to take over the house while I planned the colours and the furnishings. When the keys were handed over, I was already prepared with paints and brushes, and I started right away. I painted from early morning to late night and completely forgot to eat, it was so fun to watch the rooms take shape with the colours I wanted. Now I didn't need anyone's approval, I had wanted to paint our home for many years, but I kept hearing it was good enough as it was. After a month of work, I was able to unpack the furniture and put everything in its place, my new home was taking shape and the universe had been very generous. I was extremely grateful. My now ex-husband helped me all the way, fortunately we were good friends and wanted the very best for one another. The love we always had for each other continued, but now in a different form and he will forever be a part of the family, and so it is.

Our mutual friends were gone, but the few good friends I had with the same interests as me could now be nurtured. In the past our schedule had been filled with activities and social gatherings, so life became calmer. Autumn started its entrance, and I lit the fireplace every night. Looking into the fire while resting my mind became my favourite part of the day, now I had time to meditate, listen to spiritual conversations on youtube, or read interesting books. It was like opening a Pandora's box, the more I found the more there were to open. It was like I was finally released from my cage, and I jumped and bounced with pure joy. Why hadn't I done this sooner? Was this what I had been afraid of? Although such thoughts came up now and then I knew it was perfect timing, it happened exactly the year it was supposed to, and my good feelings was just confirmation that I had chosen what was right for me.

One day my daughter came to visit, and she asked if I had heard about ayahuasca. "No," I replied, "what is it?" When she began to talk I listened carefully, there was something hitting a spot inside of me and I became very curious. As soon as she left, I started searching for the phenomenon on google. The only plant-based medicine I knew was homeopathy, but this was something else entirely. The more I read and listened to those who had tried it the more I felt it was calling me, it felt as if there was a magnet in front of me sucking me in with great force. I finally decided to go to a retreat. When the decision was made, the next step was to find a safe place to go. I understood that many places weren't pure in intention, and I became aware of the unpleasant experiences that could be downright dangerous. There were those who pretended to be shamans to lure in foreigners and make money from ignorance. I sent up a call to be sent to authentic healers, this was too serious for me to go blindly into.

The universe didn't take long to respond, and I went online to check it out. The centre I had received a tip about had been in operation for nine years. An American, after staying in the jungle for many years, had started the place. He was clearly concerned about safety, so we had to send in an application to be approved, there were several pages of questions to map both medical and psychological backgrounds. They also had a school where they taught people about the organic cultivation of vegetables and herbs. This testified to a serious policy, so I found the courage and submitted the papers. A rush went through me when I thought about being deep in a jungle, what if there were a lot of snakes and spiders? Of course, they were a part of a place like that, but would I encounter them? Those were the worst reptiles I could meet, and I sent a prayer of grace. Even that couldn't keep me away, I had a deep knowing that this was right, and I waited in great anticipation for the response.

A week passed before I got the feedback, and I took a deep breath as I opened the mail: I got approved. The joy and excitement made my body tremble, now there was no turning back. Even though I had been to many places around the world this was completely different: no electricity and internet and far from society. In the pictures I could see dense vegetation around the simple cabins, and I was going to be with natives who had a completely different mindset than we had in the western world. I read what I could find about it and was also sent a lot of information which was important to know before I arrived. Among other things it was necessary to follow a strict diet in the last month to clean the body. Oh, how I was looking forward to this. I made a big ring on the calendar, and thought it was way too far away. The first retreat with a vacant spot wasn't until three months later, but considering the rainy season it was perfect. January was about to end, and I was due to leave on the first of May. I would use the time for preparation, physically and mentally. It was as if something had changed inside me, not anything I could put my finger on, but there was something.

Dreams have always been important to me, and as far back as I can remember they have come to show me which direction to take or to give me new perspectives. After the registration was a fact, the dreams intensified in strength and frequency, and I started to wake up during the night or early in the morning with something they had shown to me. One morning I was abruptly filled with the full knowledge of how we create time, so I jumped up from my bed as soon as I became conscious, ran down to the living room and picked up my notebook and a pen. I didn't even take the time to put on the coffee machine for fear of missing out, trying to keep all other thoughts away. I wanted to get it written down on paper while I could still see it. Another time I had woken up in the middle of the night with a knowledge of how remote healing works. This time I just lay in bed feeling how obvious it was, and that I knew this already, it was so clear and natural that I thought it wasn't necessary to write it down until the next morning, so I went back to sleep, something I should never have done. The next morning, I remembered my thoughts, but I didn't remember a single thing from the dream. Where did the clarity of knowledge go? Everything had felt so natural, I knew this from ages ago, so how could this knowing be completely removed from my mind now? I was resentful with myself for not writing down some notes, but I could do nothing about it, hopefully it would come back. I gave myself a promise never to think that I would remember without writing down some key words.

When I was shown how time is created, I saw that it all happens through the synapses in the brain. I saw it done through events and images being placed in a database in the brain, one happening after the other. It looked like an explosion of light, just like when pictures were taken with the first cameras on the market. The incident was then archived and the feeling inside the experience was memorised with the picture. The feeling was passed on through nerves being activated inside the body while the archive of images remained in the limbic system of the brain. The next event was recorded in the same way, and the next, and the next, and the next. These events were then connected by the occurrence of synapses. I understood through this process that we created a story which we could remember, because everything was connected. The feeling of time came when one event was superimposed on the next and connected. When we are remembering past events, we automatically conclude that we also have a future. *Voilà*, time is a reality. It seemed so easy when I saw it this way. The experience I had when I was waking up was the full knowledge of how it works, but it wasn't easy to find the words right away. As soon as I switched from the right brain over to the left to describe, the dream began to dissolve. I tried to write as fast as I could, it was like getting a big ball of knowledge threaded down over my head outside time, and this ball would then be transformed into a line of words *in* time. Everything was so simple, but the words would complicate it all, so I had to picture it before using words. I wondered why this knowledge had been shown to me. I am an inquisitive person, but I wouldn't even have thought of asking questions about this at the time.

Everyday life was full of activities, but completely different than before. Now it was only me who chose how I would manage my time, and I was also lucky enough to manage the working days according to my own schedule. Mornings and afternoons could be disposed of without having to consider anything other than the clients' schedules and my own needs. I probably could have done the same thing earlier, but my strong conscience had got in the way, I was always considering other people's needs first, and if there was some spare time I could use that for myself. This is what I learned growing up. When the kids were small it was necessary to let their needs be met before my own, but I hadn't learned how to stop this way of thinking. My favourite thing now was to light up the fireplace, put on low pleasant music and sit staring into the flames where my mind often wandered down to the jungle and what awaited me there.

One night when I was sitting like this in my own world, I heard some noises and my ears pricked up, someone was tripping across the floor, and it sounded like shoes with heels. I went to see what it could be, but I didn't see anyone. Back in my chair I heard it again and this time I heard it like glass clinking in the kitchen closet. "Who is here?" I said it out loud even though I knew there wasn't anybody in the room. When the sounds began, I had been thinking about my mother, "is it you mom?" When I said it out loud, I felt a cold wind against my arms, and the feeling of 'someone' coming around me was strong. "Are you really here now?" I was surprised to say the least, she had never made herself known after she died so what made her suddenly appear? "If it is you," I spontaneously said, "will you take my hand?" My arm stretched out on its own and the image of the little girl jumping and bouncing happily next to her mother on their way to town, appeared before me. "Not only am I going to take you by the hand," I heard inside me, "I also want to give you a warm hug." It felt like a cold ball around my hand and a gentle wind coming around my body, at the same time I was enveloped by a motherly love I had never known before. Is this how it feels, I thought, as I enjoyed this new feeling, the only mother's love I knew was for my own children, but now it poured towards me. I felt all my pores drinking it like nectar, no words were needed, only the feeling of closeness. "Are you okay where you are?" When I asked, I felt a joy rippling through me so strong that I had to laugh as if she was dancing around in the living room. The next moment she was gone while the sweetness of motherly love circulated in the room after the visit as if a light veil was lingering on my skin.

Destiny

After this experience I felt that a new peace had emerged inside me, and even though it was a couple of months until I was going, the impatience disappeared, now I could enjoy the excitement of being on my way. I was soon going to go on a diet and started to become more aware of what I was eating. There were many restrictions including completely avoiding sugar and fat for the last two weeks. I started reading the table of contents of the items I was buying, and I realised that most of what was pre-prepared in the store contained a lot of sugar. To cut down as much as possible I started baking myself. It was fun to compare my cart with others which I never had done before, and when I got to the checkout, I had a load of vegetables and fruit while others came with pizza, soda, and half-fabricated food in their carts. I could still eat chicken and turkey, but usually I chose vegetarian food. After a short time, my body felt much lighter, I had more energy and even my mood wasn't so fluctuating, the wellbeing it gave me came surprisingly fast and my body enjoyed this new lightness. Perhaps this participated in the frequency and clarity of my lucid dreaming, like they felt more like I was in my conscious awake state than in a normal dream. It felt as if the energy could be used in a better way when the body was not stuffed with sugar and heavy food. One of those dreams I can clearly see before my eyes just thinking about it, it is like I am there.

I suddenly become aware I am walking in the woods, and it is in the middle of the night. I know where I am heading, and I walk with firm steps along the path. It is a beautiful night, the air is clear and fresh, but not cold, the sky is packed with stars, and they shine and twinkle, so it is easy to see where I am going. After a few moments I arrive at a glen where I see five people sitting around a fire. They are wearing brown monks' robes with their hoods pulled slightly in front of their faces. I can only see the figures, but it feels like I know who they are. All of them have lanterns placed next to them, but they are not lit. They are expecting me, we agreed to this meeting a long time ago. When they see me approaching one of them stands up and walks towards me. They make room for me to sit down in the circle around the fire. They start talking, but I can't hear what they are saying, their voices are muffled and cannot reach my ears. We stay for some time while the darkness of the night creeps close. He who received me suddenly stands up and signals the lanterns to be lit, they have one each, but I didn't receive any. He gives me a sign to follow, and we all begin to walk into the woods. A path emerges between the trees, and we walk slowly upwards. The vegetation is dense, and I can feel branches scrape against my skin as I keep my eyes fixed on the lights hovering in front of me. The darkness of the night became total when we entered the forest so I must keep my eyes on the lights in front of me.

We walk for quite a while before everyone stops and turns towards me whilst they point to something I cannot see. I focus into the darkness and now I can see we have stopped next to a mountain where I can glimpse the entrance of a cave. One of them looks at me and I can hear his voice clearly: "Now we are going through this tunnel, and we will light up with our lanterns, so you don't have to be afraid, just follow the light, we will take care of you." They have an aura of safety around them, so I have no fear, and I notice a strong feeling of determination rising in me. We start to walk into the tunnel where they all walk in front of me. The surface feels rough and uneven, so we walk slowly at times. The air is perfectly still, and I can hear rattling sounds, perhaps from bats, I think, and shiver. I am not sure what the sounds indicate, and I start to feel some fear creeping in. I shift my focus to the lights swinging in front of me, thinking it is best not to listen too much to the sounds. We walk and walk, and I wonder how long this tunnel can be. Finally, I feel a small gust of wind against my cheek, and I can glimpse a spot of light far in the distance. I give a sigh; we are getting near the exit. I move on with renewed strength and the light increases in size and brightness which is reassuring. What awaits me out there, I wonder, eager to arrive.

When we reach the opening, I step out on a mountain ledge, and I become speechless at the panorama in front of me. I am in awe. It looks like I am standing inside a crater except that all the walls are chalk white, above I can see the sun is shining from a clear blue sky illuminating it all with an intensity that takes my breath away. Below there is a lake so crystal clear that I can see every detail at the bottom. I look down to the left and the most beautiful woman I have ever seen appears standing on a mountain ledge closer to the water. Her olive-coloured skin glistens in the sun, and her long black hair flows down to her lower back like a waterfall, she wears nothing, and the figure is like a sculpture in its perfect design. As I admire the radiance I sense from her, she takes a perfect plunge into the water. I can see that she is heading towards a small opening which I haven't noticed before; a narrow tunnel goes through a large rock at the bottom of the crater where she slips through like an eel and comes out of the water again. Oh, what if she had missed the opening, I shudder at the thought. While this thought runs through my head the realisation comes with the knowing that it is her confidence which is causing her to perfectly hit every time; if she had doubted the outcome she would have failed. The certainty and understanding of this truth sink deep into me.

The next moment I am in the water, and it feels like silk against my skin while I find myself diving and playing as only a little child can do.

81

I can feel the presence of my guide and we are like dolphins frolicking in freedom. The pleasure is total, a delight I have never known before is making me laugh out loud in pure joy, it is so easy to move in the clear, warm water. Every time I come to the surface, I feel connected to everything around me, the mountainsides glistening in the sun, the sky, and the water I frolic inside, even the sunbeams feel like waves of laughter, like the sun rejoices with me in the joy that ripples through my whole being.

I didn't want to wake up, I wanted to hold on to the playful freedom I had felt in the dream. Was this what I was heading towards? The five people dressed in robes seemed so real, I knew that this meeting was preplanned and I knew they were known to me. Who were they? Why couldn't I hear what was being said when we sat around the fire? What did they say and why didn't I get to know what they said? The feeling of fate came in strongly, was it really the case that it was predestined I was going to the jungle? When I walked in the woods, I had no doubt that there was a certain goal I was heading towards, and when I approached the fire, I knew that they were waiting for me. This was an agreed meeting, there was no doubt, and I knew that it had been decided a long time ago, before my coming to earth. I stored the dream in my heart, and I brought it with me as a treasure.

Guardian Angels

After this dream the impatience returned, I wanted to finish the tunnel I walked through in the dream, and bathe in the freedom I had felt. The feeling when I woke up had been indescribably delicious, so if this was the result of the healing journey I was about to enter, I could go through anything. Winter began to let go and the birds were returning with their songs of spring accompanying what was growing inside me, we were in total harmony. I counted the days while cleaning the garden from last year's leftovers, read, or meditated, and the clients rushed in, it was like a new force had taken hold of everything I did. All parts of life went smoothly, why hadn't life been like this all along, what made everything feel so easy now? I kept wondering.

The dreams continued and the meditations became more rewarding than ever. I became aware of a contact with my inner self which I hadn't noticed before as if layer after layer was cleared away, giving access to parts of myself I hadn't been conscious of before. Even though I am highly sensitive I now encountered something else as if obstacles I didn't know were there suddenly disappeared. In one of the dreams, I stood in front of a row of white, translucent curtains waving in the wind. I saw several rows of these curtains, one behind the other, all fluttering with graciousness in the warm breeze while glimpses of nature's green background emerged as the warm wind moved the curtains back and forth. It felt just like that, like something fleetingly showed up before it was gone again.

One afternoon became very different from what I had expected. Work went on smoothly and it was a bright, sunny day, one of those early days of spring demanding me to be outside. My plan was really to continue gardening, watching how the warmth from the sun made the buds on the bushes bounce, eager and overjoyed to come out. I made myself a cup of tea to enjoy the outdoor weather before I started and found a warm place in the sun where I sat down comfortably in the chair. The warmth on my face made me sigh pleasantly and I closed my eyes and sank into a relaxed doze.

Something catches my attention without me seeing what it is, it feels as if the senses can notice something I am not conscious of, and my focus gets strengthened. A vibrating light pulls me upwards like a magnet as if I am drawn to the sun far in the distance. I let myself surrender. The light changes and becomes alive, it feels like I am being consumed and am becoming one with what I am seeing. A joyous feeling ripples through my body like I am greeted by something that has been waiting for me for a long time. Lights of gold and white are dancing around me while tears of longing run silently down my cheeks, it feels like I have finally returned home.

Amid this joy of reunion, I am made aware of my heart and get a feeling that my gaze is turning downwards to find it. The moment I look down I begin to fall; I am pulled further and further away from the fluorescent light, and I can see it is getting smaller and smaller in size whilst at the same time darkness starts to envelop me. When the darkness is complete all goes quiet, the falling stops and I look around in surprise. Where did the magical light go? I tried to find it again and now I can see the darkness is divided into many shades, several semicircles in different shades become visible in front of me, some are quite bright, while others look denser, divided in different shades of grey. Now I see there is a very clear light shining between each layer. I look at the panorama in front of me while listening to the silence, knowledge that this is in my heart sinks in, this is how my heart looks from the inside. I heave a sigh of relief, feeling reassured by the light I see around all the semicircles. I know that the clear light comes from God, He knows what is going to take place and I feel safe, I know I am being watched and that I am protected.

The feeling that time has come sinks in, now is the time to heal my heart. I realise that all the grey shades represent different pains it had had to experience, layer upon layer they have built up shadows from stories and events that have occurred during my life. I feel grateful that this is revealed whilst at the same time I am wondering what secrets each one is holding on to. I search the darkness right in front of me, hold my breath and dive into it, deep inside. The darkness feels total, and my senses sharpen, a feeling comes crawling in and takes over my being: grief, a great sorrow emerges. It is so heavy it is like I cannot hold it. I can see the heart lying in front of me in a thousand pieces, whilst many angels are gathered around. I can see that they hold the pieces together. Even if they support and look after them, I can clearly see the wounded edges and scars. The angels have been here all along, I know, but now I must go in and heal my heart myself, the time has come for it to be completely restored. I need help with this, it is a task too big for me to do alone. I take the heart in my hands and reach it upwards: "God," I cry, "You have to help me heal my heart." I feel that it is being picked up, it is safe. My breath becomes deep as my consciousness returns to the now, slowly I come back to myself.

I got up off my chair and walked in, the sun had disappeared behind a cloud and the air was still a little crisp now that the heat from it was gone. I wanted to write down what had happened even if it was not possible to put it into words or to forget such an experience. The dream that had disappeared the following morning had been a strong reminder of how easily my mind could displace something it didn't want me to remember. When my heart had been picked up, I was left with a silence as if it were now time to take it easy and think as little as possible. The experience stayed with me for a long time, and it felt as if the thoughts were prevented from getting stuck in my head, everyday life floated imperceptibly by while my whole body waited for what was coming.

There were three weeks left until departure so my focus was on everything I couldn't eat, I had already reduced coffee to only one or two cups in the morning. What I dreaded was not using salt, how could I taste the food without it? We were allowed to use natural spices, but no e-substances or anything spicy so I had to make everything from scratch. No one dared to ask me to dinner during this time, but I thought it was fun to mix groceries and make all sorts of new recipes. I made many different compositions and I felt it was good to eat these organic and vegetarian dishes as if my body and I became much better friends after my diet changed.

The last night at home before leaving, I discovered that there were no extra batteries for the headlight I was bringing with me to the jungle. Since there were no charging options, I wanted to at least bring an extra set, a power bank was fully charged so I had an opportunity to charge my phone if in need. Even though I wasn't going to use the phone, it was good to bring it along. I put on my shoes and half ran down to the supermarket, it was right before closing time, so I had to be fast if I was going to make it. As I rounded the corner of the store something made me stumble and I fell forward. Now I will end up in the hospital, I thought, as everything went into slow motion. The pavement made of cement in front of the entrance got closer and closer, so I reached both my hands forward to make the fall softer, they hit the cement at the same time as my forearms prepared the strength needed to protect my face from hitting the ground. To avoid as much damage as possible I turned my nose upwards, and I resisted all that my muscles could manage. Slowly but surely, I felt my chin getting closer to the concrete and when it happened, I felt a small thump. I stayed completely still to check my condition while time normalised and I came back to myself.

A couple heading towards their car parked next to me came running over and wondered if they should drive me to the hospital. They reached out to help me get up, but I just looked at them and shook my head as I curled myself up into a sitting position. "Thank you very much," I said, slightly confused, "but I think I am okay," I had to sit until I was totally present again. They made sure that this was really the case before leaving. As I walked home, I wondered about the experience of everything going into slow motion, this was a new experience. How could time suddenly stretch out indefinitely? I went through each sequence and became aware of a feeling that something had been slowing the fall, something that wouldn't be possible to spot at a normal pace. I had seen the concrete coming towards me while I had had plenty of time to think of how to prepare my landing with as little damage as possible.

When my hands hit the ground, I found it strange that I hadn't been able to avoid my chin hitting the ground as I had all the time in the world to gather strength, so what had happened? I remembered that I was sure I would be able to stop while my face was getting closer and closer to the ground. What really made me fall? That too was a mystery. One tip of the shoe had stuck the edge of the decking in front of the store, but it was only a few millimeters high, if I tried to stumble the same way on purpose, I don't think I would have been able to do so. Well, with everything that had been happening over the last few months, after I signed up for the retreat, this was just another strange thing that I couldn't explain. I sent a 'thank you' to my guardian angels for being there and protecting me, had the fall not been slowed down I could have risked some teeth being damaged or worse. I would have ended up in hospital and not been able to leave the next day, and that would have been the worst thing ever. Now I could go with only a bruise on my chin and sore hands.

My guardian angel had stepped in once before that I know of, probably on several other occasions as well. One of the times happened nine months before the experience in 1991, when I had decided to leave this world as it felt like the only way to solve my difficulties. I believed seriously that my children and family would be better off without me, and I was convinced there were no other solutions. Everything was prepared, the letter had been written where I explained why I did it, and all the sleeping pills from the new package I had been given by my doctor were in my hand. I reached for the glass of water, but then got an idea to lie down on the couch, I had to have one last review of my thoughts. The only thing I remembered afterwards was that I lay my head on the pillow and then everything went black.

The next moment, as I opened my eyes, the sun flooded in. At first, I was totally confused, and I had to gather myself back to the environment before I sat up. I looked at the letter and felt the horror take hold of me, last night's experiences were racing through my mind and caused me to yell out loud. What was I thinking of, what did I almost do? The children could have been motherless at this exact moment, I shuddered at the thought as if a new clarity had come in. I let the night's thoughts circulate, and as I looked at them, I decided never to sink that deep again. It felt like a sacred promise, and I knew that this was how it would be, something had changed radically inside me, and I could feel a strength coming forth, one that wasn't there when I made the preparations last night.

I thanked my guardian angel and started looking for all the pills, convinced I would find them on the couch or on the floor around where I had been lying. After I had crawled around and searched for quite a while, I found them spread around the entire living room, they must have been forcibly thrown to reach the other side of the room. I remembered nothing after I had lain my head on the pillow as if I had been put into a deep sleep. After every tablet was found, as was very important because the kids could believe they were candies, I sat down. I felt the new strength and determination that I would be able to do whatever I had to do, from now on a lot would change.

As I strolled up the hill I began to wonder if there were forces out there which didn't want me to go to the jungle. Well, I thought, then they shall find resistance. I thought of the meditation where my heart was picked up by God and the dream where I met the five monks, what was destined to occur no one could prevent, but they could try. I felt a deep gratitude knowing I was looked after: you guys around me don't have much free time, I had to smile to myself at the thought. Once back home I packed the last toiletries and went straight to bed, the plane would depart at six in the morning and first transit was in Amsterdam. The next bed I was going to lie down on would be in Iquitos, Amazon here I come! I drifted into sleep with a smile on my face.

The Jungle

A heat filled with humidity struck me as I stepped off the plane in Iquitos. The trip had gone smoothly with all departures and arrivals as announced, and the long leg from Amsterdam to Lima had gone surprisingly fast. I had been dreading twelve hours in a cramped airplane seat, but with good books and music in my ears the hours had passed like a breeze. It was delightfully liberating to let go of all thoughts of duties and responsibilities and to go inside without worrying about having to do anything. Now the journey was behind me, knowing that the next morning we would be picked up for the travel into the bush. I hailed a motor taxi, which is a moped with a carriage behind, and went to the hotel.

It was a colourful view, the mopeds swung quickly between cars while the passengers clawed their way to avoid rolling out of the vehicle. The security was way different, not what we are used to considering. It looked like a whole family could fit onto two wheels, the wife in the back, preferably with a small child between herself and the driver, and several children in front. There was honking and waving, and along the way I could see stalls where they sold vegetables and fruit or someone cooking in large pots. The buildings were a mix of brick houses and sheds, and on a long brick wall I saw a couple of young adults painting a beautiful drawing. My first impression was of a vibrant community where people gestured, chatted, and laughed. This is an environment where I feel at home after living several years in Spain, and I smiled to myself as the warm wind blew my hair in all directions.

The hotel was good, but very spartan. I felt a little sorry for the poor boy who carried my (too) heavy bag up several flights of stairs, of course my room had to be on the top floor. After showering and changing into more summery robes I strolled out into the city. I sat down at a small café and ordered the world's best pineapple juice I have ever tasted. Unfortunately, I wasn't aware that I had to order without sugar, but it tasted heavenly. In my naivety I had thought that they would only serve ayahuasca-friendly juices, but I learned quickly. I felt uplifted afterwards so maybe that was what I had needed after a long journey and some jet lag.

The town was enormous, but after a short walk I came to a beautiful, paved promenade running along the Lago Moronacocha, a tributary river of the Amazon. The promenade was located high in the terrain and the view of the buildings alongside the river was fantastic. I could see a jumble of plank huts built on piles so that the floods during the rainy season would not destroy them and they were built into each other. There were several rows of huts, and it was a motley assembly to watch while I walked along the promenade, I was told later that about five thousand people lived in these simple huts. It was a great panorama, so I stayed for a long time watching people working or sitting outside doing their things. I tried to imagine what it would be like to grow up in such a place, it was so totally different from home, one thing that seemed obvious was that there wasn't much room for privacy here. A couple of years later there was a fire in the area where one of the healers I had got to know, a beautiful and gentle woman in her early forties, lost everything she owned. Donations were arranged through the centre and sent down to help her get back on her feet, and I hope everything is good with her now. It is a great tragedy when such things happen in an environment like this, fires will spread quickly, and people don't have a lot with which to rebuild their losses.

I continued the walk and saw groups of women dressed in the distinctive garments of the Shipibo tribe, they are one of the original tribes of the rainforest and they have a strong tradition of healing abilities. The knowledge of plants and their healing properties has been passed on for generations through thousands of years. I soaked up the smells and the atmosphere as I strolled further up the river, the heat quivered, but the breeze made it possible to walk around without getting too hot. Along the way I was stopped by young men who asked if I was interested in ayahuasca ceremonies. Since we were warned about this, I just replied that I already had a place I was attending, and they quickly disappeared. It was a relief to stretch my legs after twenty-four hours in airplane seats and I enjoyed walking by myself.

Back at the hotel I had an early dinner to be well rested until the next day. I glanced at some foreigners sitting nearby and wondered if they were going to the same place. There was one man by himself, and I was on the of verge asking him, but my courage failed, I had learned not to disturb anyone, so I stayed sitting neatly on my chair. It was heavenly to be able to stretch out my whole body when I crawled into bed, and rushes of anticipation chased through me while sleep imperceptibly lulled me into its veil.

The next morning, I woke up early. In a few hours I would be in the jungle. The thoughts of everything I had dreamt of and experienced over the last months made me extra excited about what the next two weeks would bring. I was as ready as I could be and grabbed a light breakfast which was not as diet friendly as I would have hoped, it was clear that people preferred cakes and sweet supplements in the morning, but they did have some fruit and rolls. When I entered the reception many people in the group who were going out into the jungle with me had already arrived. The heat outside was burning hot, it was as if the air was standing still and I could see it rise from the ground in torrents, inside the air conditioning went haywire while everyone did their utmost to deafen it.

The conversations were lively between the people who knew each other and those who didn't, there weren't many people travelling by themselves, most of them had brought a partner or a friend. The person sitting alone at dinner the night before was sitting on the couch gesturing, so I could have made contact the evening before. The atmosphere was open and light, and I learned that people had come from many parts of the world: Germany, England, Australia, Portugal, and several places in America were represented. It was mostly young people, but some were fortunately around my age and even older, I breathed a sigh of relief and stood in this motley congregation with a good feeling. Many of them I would never have contacted without such a gathering, but now I was far outside my usual surroundings, and I was more alive than ever before. Everyone was exceptionally friendly, so I made good contacts with several of them in this first meeting. During the next two weeks we would get to know each other as though we had been friends for years.

When the bus arrived, which was supposed to take us to the port, my eyes opened wide, could this thing carry us all the way? It reminded me of the buses in circulation when I was a child, and it looked like it had been used for all those years too. Our luggage was stowed on the roof and fastened with lashes of thick ropes; a tarpaulin was duly fastened to protect from any downpours of rain as the weather could change from one moment to the next. I was seated in the front row and had a good view of what was going on. The bus honked and coughed before the driver made it start after several attempts, then we drove about ten meters before it stopped again, right in the middle of an intersection. They pushed it out of the intersection and started to look at the engine, and after a bit of back and forth they got it started again and the trip could continue. The door had to be closed manually and the assistant was standing halfway inside the bus and half outside it, there wasn't a lot of air conditioning, so I was grateful for the air pouring in. The heat was intense, but I enjoyed the feeling and smell of warm, moist soil, every now and then the scent of food and spices came from the stalls along the way, and I sniffed it up with gusto.

A cloud of dust surrounded the bus when we came out of the city center and left behind the concrete roads, for the rest of the trip the roads consisted of hard-trodden red soil and the bus swerved from side to side to avoid the biggest holes in the streets. The motor taxis were everywhere, either with tourists in the carriage or with whole families, the homes I saw along our journey alternated between cozy little houses where the garden was nicely planted, and sheds where there was everything from cookware to old, worn-out mopeds outside. Children were running around together, some wearing only shorts while others were dressed in their school uniform. It was a lively and colourful spectacle watching all that was going on along the road and I enjoyed every moment of it. The trip to the docks took about an hour and a half and I was impressed that the bus managed the whole way. There had been dirt roads since we left Iquitos and for the most part buildings on the sides. A few rain showers caused them to turn on windshield wipers that had probably seen better days five years ago, here they took care of everything as long as there was still a bit of utility in them.

Those who picked us up carried all the luggage and put it into one of the boats while we were told to go into another. The boy who steered the boat was standing behind with the rudder in his hand and another boy was sitting in front to check that there was nothing in the water that could ruin the motor. This was the Amazon River itself and it was wide and winding, just as I have seen from the airplane. We slipped out of the harbour and followed the river for a while before we continued into a tributary where the river narrowed considerably. I saw a cluster of houses on the banks we were passing and wondered what it was like to live there. The houses had straw roofs and were located inside a wide, open area with the rainforest surrounding them. I could see children running around playing with a flock of brown chickens pecking around between them. Smaller boats with outboard motors kept passing by, some led by very young children, and I understood that this was the most common means of transport they used.

We drove through reeds and rounded a bend where the river became very narrow and branches from bushes and trees bumped into the boat, it was fascinating to see all the flowers and plants, many of which had their roots in the water. Eventually it became clear that we had to sneak our way forward, the rainy season had just finished, and everything changed from day to day due to the weather. We had been told that the trip could take anywhere from half an hour to two hours depending on how the river behaved. It was now getting more and more shallow, and the big boat couldn't get any further. Smaller boats approached us, and we climbed into them to be able to go further in, the last fifty meters from shore even they had to stop too, as the river was too shallow, and we were told to walk the rest. I wondered how this would turn out, weren't there piranhas in these waters? I was glad I had brought my wilderness boots as they covered me up to my hip. What about snakes and crocodiles or other unknown creatures? I trod carefully getting out of the boat and was relieved that the water only reached to my knees, the extra protection from the boots was reassuring as I slowly walked towards the shore, the others had sport shoes or short rain boots, so I was glad to have mine.

At the shore they had made an area where they received guests and kept the boats while they were not in use. I was looking at the others coming safely in and changing their footwear before we were able to continue our journey on land. Many young boys were waiting for us to carry our luggage and I felt so sorry for the one who had to carry mine, I was embarrassed that I hadn't considered this point when I had bought the bag. Most of the others only had one backpack and here I came with a huge travel bag, the wheels were of no support when there were no roads. The boy swung it up on his shoulder and trotted along the path as if it weighed nothing. I looked around while we were going, and it was fascinating to know that we were now deep in the jungle. The road was like a narrow country road with two-wheel tracks and grass in the middle. A few swarms of butterflies were frightened by the noise we created and flew up like a small cloud of yellow wings, I had to stop to admire the sight. We walked past an opening with a few houses, one of them under construction, where I could see the laundry swaying in the wind and several chickens running around cackling. When I saw the place, I had a feeling of déjà vu as if it were a familiar sight. The thought of spiders and snakes was far away, I felt just as safe to walk here as in a densely populated area at home. After a forty-five-minute walk I saw the gate to the retreat site, and on the other side of the gate I could see a welcoming committee had gathered to greet us. They were all dressed in the Shipibo suits, and one by one we walked through the gate where everyone was present to receive us, from the cleaners and the workers in the field, to the healers; I had arrived.

Tambo Number 7

After a warm welcome we were told they wanted to give us a flower bath before they showed us to the cabins, the tambos. I had to find my bikini as they wanted to cleanse us of all the dust before we could move around. A flower bath was made with water filled with petals from various flowers, which they had prepared in large bowls. The aroma was the best I had ever smelled, and they used small tubs to pour the water over the whole body. Even though I had to hold my breath when the cold water flowed over my warm skin, it gave me a magical feeling, like rejuvenation. Just the memory of this makes me want to go back. We were not allowed to use towels afterwards; it was important for the water to dry on the body so that the essences of the flowers could penetrate the pores. I was full of these little flowers in many colours and breathed in the scents from them with pleasure. Afterwards we gathered in the maloka where we were assigned our own tambo. A maloca is a gathering place where all ceremonies and group gatherings are held, it is built according to the principles of sacred geometry and they are always round or oblong, and the roof is a network of logs where palm leaves are attached to provide shelter from the weather. Wherever we travel in South America we will find the same structures.

I walked behind the boy carrying my bag and was excited about where I would end up, the cabins were scattered around the area, and some were placed at a short distance from the centre. I hoped mine wouldn't lie too far away as I would have to walk through solitary areas by myself. After a few minutes of walking, it appeared between palm trees and bushes as if it were all by itself. It felt like it was welcoming me, and my heart smiled when I saw the number seven, I loved that number and I had had many dreams where the number appeared. All cabins had a half-enclosed area where a dry toilet was located together with a small sink with a water tank above. This was an unexpected luxury. In addition, it contained a double bed with a mosquito net, a desk, a bookshelf, and a hammock. I felt at home right away and I started to unpack some small things to make it cozy, my clothes were left in the bag safely wrapped in plastic bags with zip-locks due to the humidity, and it also felt a little safer when I was sure that no small insects could hide between the layers. On my desk I put the notebook I had bought for the occasion, an icon of Saint Mary I had brought from home and the flashlight. When all were prepared for the evening, I went to look for the others.

I went over to the dining room where all were gathered, and we were served a delicious lunch. Everything was so orderly, there was no doubt that they wanted the best for everyone who was visiting and that their policy was to provide a good service. There were several tables around the room and a small section where a bookshelf was filled with books others had left behind. The water can, from which we could fill our water bottles, was placed next to a pillar in the middle of the room, and a mesh door led out to a small balcony that was protected by mosquito nettings. The talk was lively, and the atmosphere was friendly and inviting. My thoughts went to all the trips I had been on, all the suites I had stayed in, and none of them had ever given me the pleasant feeling of belonging which was registering in me now. There were young adults with singlets and tattoos on most of their bodies, other adults with more familiar clothing styles, some were very stylish with shawls draped around them and me in my ordinary robes. It was a good mix, and everyone came for the same reason: wanting a happier life and improved health. Eventually I got to hear a lot of life stories, and I felt a lot of gratitude and respect to them for being so openhearted, some had been there before, but for most of us it was our first time.

After the meal we gathered in the maloca again where all the shamans and assistants briefly introduced themselves, then it was our turn and we presented ourselves and shared where we came from and the intention for coming. We were twenty-three participants, so the presentation went on for the rest of the afternoon, just in time for a light dinner for those who wanted some more food before we went our separate ways. Finally, it was time for relaxation, the day had been packed with new experiences and impressions, so I needed to soak it all in. The night came quickly and by the time I was back in the tambo it was already pitch dark. I could see the stars shining between the palm leaves on my way back and the Milky Way was glittering far up in the night sky. The sounds were many and unfamiliar so I shone around in nooks and crannies with my flashlight to make sure there were no spiders or snakes in the cabin. Every time I went to the bathroom, I scrutinised my surroundings with a critical eye and when I got into bed, I wrapped the mosquito net tightly around the mattress to be sure nothing could enter. I lay in the dark listening to the sounds of crickets and frogs choking and the rustling of palm leaves. I had some bats as my closest neighbours and I could hear how they flew around catching food and squealing, it was like lying outside in their midst, which I did with only a mosquito net, or two, separating us. At the same time as it was new and unfamiliar, I felt a calmness come over me and fell into a deep sleep while the bats worked diligently outside.

The next morning, I woke up at six o'clock and watched the darkness of the night gradually being replaced by daylight. I quickly put on my summer dress, after shaking it, and went over to the dining room to get a cup of tea. Everything was quiet, but I saw people already working around in the area. Here it was customary to go to bed when the sun set and to get up at dawn, at noon it was too hot to work so they used the hours with the lowest temperature for outdoor activities. Butterflies whirled around the beautiful flowers and the sounds from the bush seemed different now. The scents of exotic plants were intense in the morning hours, and I sniffed in with pleasure while my eyes wandered around. The fear of spotting something scary murmured gently in my stomach and rustling sounds drew my gaze with a quickness that even a chameleon could envy.

Eventually I had to have a serious talk with myself, I was going to be here for two weeks, so it was just a matter of getting used to these new surroundings. I realised that many grow up and live their whole lives in these surroundings and die a natural death, so it couldn't be that dangerous, could it? Vegetation was dense around the houses so it was impossible to get involved with everything that could be hidden. I strolled down to a small pond where I sat down on a bench to enjoy the atmosphere and take notes in my book. It was as if my ordinary thoughts could not exist here in this atmosphere, the sentences flowing out of the pen felt as if they lived their own lives. No interference through wi-fi or other digital gadgets abounded, just the chirping of birds and the buzzing of insects. I could have sat there for ages but was eventually joined by several others with the same intention.

At eight o'clock it was time for 'vomitivo', a cleansing of the stomach, and it was quite a process. They had boiled water with lemongrass, which we had to drink on the spot; half a litre of lukewarm water without stopping, the taste was good, but I had to have a couple of pauses to catch my breath. Afterwards we waited half a minute before we had to drink as much water as we could manage, and then some more. They said that when it started to hurt it was important to keep going, that that was when we most likely could manage to start vomiting. It was tough, but we all made it through. They followed each one of us to decide when we were cleansed, until then it was just a matter of drinking more water, I didn't really want breakfast when I had finished, to say the least. Later the individual consultations with the shamans began. I didn't get my first meeting until a couple of days later and would therefore have gone through the first two ceremonies before I had a talk with them. The day passed at a leisurely pace, but a growing pain began to take its toll on my body; my back, hips, shoulders, neck, knees, all of me began to ache more and more. Eventually it became difficult to lie in bed and relax or read, but luckily, I managed to get a nap after lunch, that evening we were going to have our first ceremony and I wanted to be rested. Strange how tired one can become without doing anything.

Ayahuasca

The time for the first ceremony approached and I felt a turmoil in my stomach creep in; what would happen during the night, and what would the medicine we were going to drink do to me? What if nothing happened? My thoughts circled as I pulled out what I wanted to bring to the maloca to make myself comfortable. It was still warm, but I knew that the evening and night could be cold, so I brought a poncho, warm shawls, and a pillow to have on my back. I tucked the pillow under my arm, put the flashlight where I could easily find it and walked with determination to my first meeting with the medicine.

Several people had already arrived, and I looked around to feel which mattress to choose, they were placed in a large ring with a pot and a roll of toilet paper in front of each. I chose one that was placed near the exit so that I could easily find my way to the toilet if I needed to. I had heard horror stories where people couldn't get out fast enough, and I didn't want to experience that at any cost, so I chose my place carefully. The mood in the room was palpable with a low hum of voices mixed with the crickets that rubbed their legs outside. I found myself a plastic chair without legs and put it on the mattress, the pain made it impossible for me to sit for a long time without support, so I was pleased that they had some of these available. The shamans, or maestros as they wanted to be called, wanted us to sit for as long as they sang, to receive icaros directly toward our bodies. If we needed to lay down, we had to get up every time that we got a personal song from the maestros.

Icaros are medicine songs which they learn from the plants. When they start on the road to becoming curanderos (healers), they have diets with one plant at a time. The essences they drink are made from the flowers, stem, or root, or from trees they want to learn from, and they take these essences into a jungle hut where they will be alone for several weeks or months. They get a small bowl of rice daily, sometimes with a piece of fish, otherwise they sit with their focus on the plant and drink a small glass every day. When they achieve contact with the spirit of the plant, a song comes forth along with the wisdom the plant contains. Plants have different abilities and can open the connection to the dream world, increase creativity, heal diseases caused by energetic blockages, open the heart or the voice and so on. When they sing different songs, they call for help from the plant's spirits. Some diets can last for several years, but then they are not alone for all that time. They can function in daily life with a strict diet and abstinence from sex. At this retreat we would get a mix of plants twice a day to enhance our intentions, what plants we needed was determined by the maestros during our personal conversations.

After an hour of light yoga and meditation I lay down on the mattress to calm my mind, but it wasn't easy to stop the chatter going on. The darkness came quickly and only a few lanterns were lit where the maestros were to settle down. They hadn't arrived yet, so I just lay there relaxing with the sounds from the outside as pleasant background music. I managed to calm my mind a little through listening to the hum of the flies and sounds from the jungle. Some mosquitoes wanted me for dinner, and I waved them away. The room was completely silent now, everyone was immersed in their own world. The round pointed roof where I could see the wooden beams placed in geometric patterns, and palm leaves neatly placed to shelter from wind and weather, was a beautiful sight. Hm, I thought, isn't it easy for all sorts of creepies to get in there? I stared with scrutinising eyes and spotted a mosquito net attached along the entire roof: whew, I could relax again. It was reassuring to rest my gaze upwards, as if protection was present, and I was relieved that I had spotted the mosquito net.

In the midst of all the unknown, I felt safe. Everything was quiet now; it was as if even nature was waiting for something. A seriousness creeped in, and I heard the maestros approaching, they were laughing and talking to each other which comforted me: maybe it wouldn't be so hard. They sat down at their seats and began the preparations, three women and two men. I watched every movement with interest and saw how the assistants made sure that everything was in place: filling up their water bottles and placing several buckets in front of the maestros. The low conversation between them as they rigged up felt like waves in the room, they emanated safety and clearly knew what they were doing. Eventually they settled down and started the actual process of the ceremony. Twenty-three pairs of excited eyes were aimed at them as they whistled gently into their pusanga bottles. Pusanga is floral water with heavenly scents which they use every time they finish singing an icaro. They take a small sip and squirt it inside our hands and over the crown of our head, to seal the job they had done. Finally, the man who was supposed to give the medicine, sang an icaro into the bottle of ayahuasca, it was so beautiful that I felt a sting in my heart. One by one we stepped forward and got the dose we were intended to have.

Since it was my first time, I only got a small amount. The assistant said that this evening was for me to get to know the medicine and for the medicine to know me, and for the maestros to diagnose my needs. I sat down in my chair and decided that I would surrender to whatever happened, it would be as it was supposed to be, I thought. When everyone had received their dose, they put out the lanterns and it became completely dark. It was time for meditation and the silence was total inside the maloca. The sounds from the crickets became very intense and close, and together with the sounds of rustling palm leaves I had a feeling of sitting in the middle of nature. After a few moments I heard coughing and uneasiness, and some people started throwing up. The medicine wasn't as bad as I had been told, but it wasn't good either. The taste filled our throats, and we weren't allowed to drink anything else after it was taken. For the last three hours we had been told not to eat or drink, which was not easy in the heat. We could rinse our mouths, but not swallow. My last meal was lunch so there wasn't much else down there now, but a little ayahuasca.

After something that felt like an eternity, they started singing, and it was incredibly beautiful to listen to. The pain in my body subsided little by little as the medicine began to work, it made it possible for me to rest in my chair and enjoy the vibration of their voices. It was a cacophony of sounds and tones. Each had his, or her own song, and together it became a beautiful choir. When I let myself sink into the sounds it felt like a memory was trying to come in, something I couldn't grasp, but it felt known to me. I tried to follow the feeling, but it was not possible to drag the memory closer. I capitulated and allowed myself to be enveloped in a good mood. The songs I received personally from each one deeply affected me. Since I know Spanish, I was able to understand many of the words, but most of the vocabulary was in their own language, one I didn't know. The love that radiated out of them was like a living river, as if it swirled around and surrounded my whole body. Here I was at home, and I felt great gratitude for having been taken into this world.

When the ceremony finished, I lay down on the mattress completely worn out. Even though not much had, in fact, happened, it felt like I had run a marathon. The ceremony lasted for five or six hours, and I was surprised at how fast the time had flown by. One of the assistants took out his guitar and started singing the most beautiful songs, and more people tuned in as time went on. What a privilege to lie here in the middle of the sounds of rustling palm leaves and beautiful music, worn out and with a sense of being at home. I couldn't go to my tambo until they had finished singing, it was like lying in a cocoon of safety and love. All the pain was gone, and I just floated with all the sounds around me, even the fear of all small or large reptiles did not exist. The mood I was led into through the medicine, the songs, and the surroundings, lulled me into a feeling of being, of presence. I wanted to rest in it as long as possible. At three in the morning, I was back in my tambo, inside the mosquito net, and fell asleep like a baby.

Raining Stars

Next morning, I was awakened by the fact that the pain had returned, now with even more intensity than the day before. When I was fourteen the sciatica pain began. Sometimes I suddenly had to stop when I was out walking, because my left foot wouldn't carry me, I was forced to stop and wait until the strength came back. I didn't understand why these ailments started, but eventually I understood that they stemmed from an accident I had had when I was ten years old. I was the first in the family to have Saturdays off from school, and since my parents were teachers, I was the only one home. We always had porridge that day, so I was given the responsibility of making it ready for when they got home. The kettle was large, and it was hard to stir all the time, one day I hadn't been good enough at stirring so the porridge burned. When my father came home and saw what had happened, he exploded in anger. I was told to go to the store to buy a new package of rice with the words: "Pity on you if you don't come home with the rice." My father's voice rang in my ears as I ran as fast as I could to get to the store before it closed. The store was on the other side of a busy road, and although I glanced quickly at both sides, I didn't see the bike coming at full speed down the hill, my glasses were fogged after the run as I was in a hurry.

It all happened in seconds, before I knew it, I woke up on the ground with a feeling of not being able to breathe. I heard someone talking to me and I started to whisper: "thump my back, thump my back," trying to get my breath back. When I managed to open my eyes I saw a man above me with a despairing expression on his face, behind him I saw a policeman taking notes in a notebook. When I was finally able sit up, my only thought was about the fact that I had to get the rice. The fear of coming home without it was bigger than the pain from the accident. The policeman wanted to take me to the hospital for a check-up and horror trickled through my body: I had to make it to the shop. I managed to convince them I was perfectly fine and ran across the road. Some young boys sat on the stairs outside the shop and watched my despair when I discovered that the door was closed, they had all been watching the incident. One of them got up and pried the door open so that I could slip in.

On my way home I met my mother and began to cry as soon as I saw her. She asked what had happened, and I answered that dad had been so angry when I burned the porridge, I had already forgotten all about the accident. Several years passed before I told anyone what had happened that day, it was somehow not present in my mind. Because of the sciatica pain, I had an x-ray taken when I was seventeen, and that showed a slight curvature of my spine on the right side, where the handlebars of the bike had hit from the left. That was when I told them what had happened to me.

Muscle tension in my shoulders and back caused me to start physical therapy when I moved back to Norway at the age of eighteen, after living in Spain for the previous two years. There I met the man who became my first husband, and we got married when I was nineteen. My first child was born the year after we married, and when he was six months old, we moved back to my then husband's hometown. Shortly after we moved to Spain, I had my first prolapse, and had to stay in bed for several days as it was too painful to move. I got the diagnosis of fibromyalgia, as previously mentioned, when I was in my mid-twenties. It was as if my body was protesting, and everything escalated in the years following. I had my fifth prolapse at the beginning of my forties, and at that time I had been having massages and visits to a chiropractor regularly for the last twenty years. In my mid-forties I also started having cramps in my back, which made me bedridden for days. Now my body hurt so much that it felt as if all the pains I had had throughout my life had come back at the same time. The only thing I could think of was getting to a civilised place where painkillers could be obtained. All of me cried out and wanted to flee.

Although these thoughts were strong, I knew no pill could help. Doctors had given me different types of pills through the years to see if they could help, but eventually I gave up. Acupuncture had the best effect on me, so I had stopped taking medication a long time ago. I walked restlessly around, sat for a bit, went to bed a bit, but couldn't find peace anywhere. I felt chewed up and spat out and just wanted to lie down and cry.

The day passed in a way, and when the time for the next ceremony was approaching, I was eager to go. When I had the medicine last night, although just a small dose, all the pain had left, and I hoped the same effect would occur this evening. I went to the maloca early to be sure of having one of the chairs, or I wouldn't be able to sit, and I lay down on the mattress. I couldn't take part in the yoga, but it was good just to be in the atmosphere and listen to the calm voice of the girl guiding. This evening I received a bigger cup, and when the medicine began to work, I felt the pain subside. I was finally able to lower my shoulders and be present with what was happening around me. The evening was different at every point, the psychedelic patterns were powerful, and I let them play out while I floated in a wealth of beautiful colours, so enchanting that I forgot everything else. After a while it got dark, as if all the lights suddenly were shut off. The images changed and a film started rolling instead of all the patterns circulating in colours.

A large, white southern house appeared at the top of a hill, and I could see beautiful green grass spreading down towards where I was standing, I got a feeling of running with small feet up to the house. The porch ran along the entire side with a wide, big staircase leading up to it, and I could see a double door where we could enter the building. I started playing next to the stairs and I saw myself as a little girl around two years old. As soon as this picture appeared I remembered the place; Oh, I thought, that is where I went every night to find love and safety. It was as if an old memory, deeply buried in my subconscious, was coming back in full force. It appeared in the same way we remember something when looking at old photos, only this was even more vivid as I experienced myself. I looked at the little girl, being her at the same time. I remembered that sometimes I played with a lot of other kids, and sometimes I was there alone. Here I felt at home and my heart leapt with joy at the instant recognition and remembrance.

Icaros sounded around the room and led me on to other lives. The beautiful woman I had seen in the dream appeared and I realised that it was me who I had seen, I remembered that I was part of an Indian tribe, and that we lived in a covenant with nature. Then a new life took over, this time from a gypsy camp. I remembered how we used to travel around in wagons, and how the unity amongst us was strong and good. The film showed me how we camped and rigged up for the night, and how we gathered around the fire, chatting and laughing. I felt the cheerful atmosphere of lively chatter and gesturing throughout me, no wonder I was fond of dancing and music, and that I felt at home in southern countries. The rhythms made us move and swing to the beat from the notes floating around using drums and flutes, guitars, and rattles. Much wisdom was imparted from mother to daughter, knowledge of plants and animals, songs we sang while we were growing crops, to use for medicine and food. Here in this environment, nature was equal to us humans, it gave us what we needed in abundance, and we conveyed our gratitude through our songs.

The memories I had felt in the distance the night before, but couldn't get hold of, poured in. It was so beautiful and joyful I felt tears in my eyes, while the movies and memories were given free rein. When everyone had received their icaro, I lay down on the mattress to rest, while the shamans continued to work. Suddenly I saw some hands approaching with a heart inside. It was whole and fresh, without any brands or scars. The heart I had given to God was now delivered back without a blemish. I reached out to receive it and placed it in my chest. The smile lit up my whole face when it fell into place, and the feeling of gratitude took over my whole existence. The second it slipped into place I heard one of the maestros do a sopla, (a powerful exhale), and realised that he was sealing the connection I had with my heart. Joy sprinkled through me, and it felt like my ears were the only thing stopping my smile going around my head. Wow, the wonderful heaviness from the heart now lying in its place, was the best heaviness I have ever felt.

On my way to my tambo I stopped at the bridge to gaze up at the sky, this spot was without too much vegetation obstructing the view upwards. In order not to fall, I had been looking down at the ground, while my flashlight lit up roots from trees and obstacles I could stumble upon. When I lifted my gaze upwards, I was left open mouthed, I was totally taken aback, mesmerised by what caught my vision. All the stars had come down to me and I reached out to touch them, that was how close they seemed. It looked like I was surrounded by trillions of stars, and they were many times bigger than had ever been seen before, I had never ever seen a night sky like this. Every star surrounding me was alive, and it felt as if they were talking to me. There were shooting stars back and forth, as if I was standing in the middle of a heavenly rain, they were sparkling and flashing like the most beautiful diamonds as they gave off their magical lights. It felt more like they were souls flying around talking with me, sharing all their wisdom, they were not just stars and never will be after this sight. Here I was at home. Amid this sea of light and power I was a part of them, and they were a part of me. It is not possible to reproduce the vision in words, but it will forever be with me and in me. I haven't had such an experience either before or since, this was a gift. The mosquitoes were starting to come close, or maybe I started to be conscious of them, I was pulled back to the world I existed in, and the thoughts of every other creepy crawly that could come out at night crept back in. Reluctantly I tore myself loose and hurried into the cabin. As I crouched under the mosquito net, I was left without a thought, but with the image of what was right outside the cabin. I slipped into sleep, as if surfing in the cosmos with the stars.

The Treasure Map of Life

When I woke up early the next morning, I just floated in a grateful beingness, the starry night sky was the first thought coming into my mind. The experience of the stars as living beings shooting back and forth in constant dialogue with me, was so strong that I had to acknowledge that they were not just something I could admire from afar anymore. They were here. As they lined up like millions of rockets around me, they felt more like souls in other dimensions. It was as if a recollection had appeared from the depths of me, providing an explosion of instant delight. The light was equal to what I had seen between the layers in my heart: it was white, translucent, transparent, and at the same time alive, as if it had its own consciousness. In all this the stars appeared as if they were dancing, and I was there with them. I stored the feeling deep inside my heart, this was way beyond what my mind could fathom, but I had the experience within.

The pain wasn't quite as bad when I got up. It was a relief to be able to stand in the shower and soap my body without having to hold my breath and force myself into every move. This day it was my turn to have a conversation with the shamans, and I was happy that I had had all the experiences first. It was like the universe was putting everything into the right order once again. After breakfast I went to the maloca to meet the group of maestros, and now I managed to sit reasonably calmly, focusing on the conversation. I shared what I had experienced at the end of the last ceremony about the heart, and asked if one of them had done a sopla. One of the men raised his hand so I asked if he had really seen my heart come back to me. When he answered in the affirmative it made me speechless, is that possible, I thought, as I looked at him in amazement, what was going on in my mind was clearly not hidden from any of them. After telling them about my pains it was decided that I would be given a massage every day after the morning medication, and I was relieved. They also agreed on which plants I should drink twice a day, to help me with the healing process.

I felt light and happy when I left them, I was in the right place, and I was confident that they could see the root of all my pains and what it would take to heal them. After years of searching, I finally felt that all of me was taken care of. No doctor understood the connection between the emotions and the physical like they did. I even had confirmation of my experience of my heart being returned, and that was important feedback for me. This anchored my belief in myself and my experiences, not just here, but also in everything that had happened at home before I came here. This confirmation lifted me up and I felt lighter in my steps than ever before. It felt as if every cell in my body was smiling when I picked up the notebook to write down everything about the meeting.

When I got down to the pond I couldn't see anyone so I could sit down in stillness, enjoying the sight in front of me. What a beautiful place this is, I thought, no wonder people come back. I contemplated a strange new feeling inside where I could allow myself to be exactly as I am, without anyone looking at me with a strange expression on their faces. This feeling was so new and pleasant I felt tears in my eyes, the notebook stayed next to me on the bench while I let this subtle and cautious sprout increase. "I can be me, and I can trust my experiences," the index finger of childhood appeared in my memory, telling me to shut down, while I said the sentence again and again.

Since we had a day off, we had a delicious dinner in the evening. The dining room buzzed with happy voices, sharing stories and experiences, there was an openness and an intimacy where it was easy to be authentic. The conversations came from the heart, the humour and the laughter were floating loosely, and we were like a family who had finally been brought together. The darkness began to descend, and lanterns were lit on all the tables. I went out on to the small patio with some of the others, and there I saw a big, blue morphidea butterfly flying around. I was stunned by the size of it. Another person made me aware of a hummingbird outside the netting, it flapped loudly as it stuck its beak into one of the flowers blooming on the trees. I stared and stared at the beautiful creature, one of the wonders of nature. The sounds of the jungle were increasing in frequency as the darkness became denser, and it was hard to tear myself away from this evening. Finally, I broke loose, so tired that I could no longer concentrate. I was looking forward to crawling into bed listening to the sounds and letting them lull me in.

Early next morning I woke up at dawn and stayed in bed to enjoy the moment. I was glad that I had gone to bed early after two long evenings and nights. To wake up almost without pain was magical, and I stayed a little longer listening to the birds chirping and the voices of workers who were already busy doing their tasks. My mind couldn't take over, I just rested with a feeling of how good life could be. I had never known such harmony and peace for as long as I could remember, perhaps not ever. Happily, I didn't know that this was the famous calm before the storm. Here I was resting in peace, enjoying the light of day as it rose, and it felt like this was how it was going to be for the rest of my life. I strolled over to the dining room and poured a cup of tea. I brought my notebook and went down to the small lake to do some writing. The other days it hadn't been possible due to pain, so now I wanted to enjoy a quiet moment with the pen in my hand. The words floated out by themselves as if they had just been waiting for me to open myself up to them.

All physical pains are a disharmony of who you are. They are manifestations of painful, negative feelings and thoughts which are not released, and they then affect the body. You are not your body, but it is your physical expression of who you are in this life. For as long as you live in it, it will guide you. It tells you if there is something you need to address, and it is your guide. For you to become aware of what stagnant energy you are holding onto, listen to your body and learn its language. You are not the experiences, but they activate the energetic system. When activated, mentally or physically, it comes from a memory which is stuck in the limbic system. This in turn is connected to the nervous system where the blockages occur. It is here where the flow of energy into the body is being impeded. When the energy is stopped, then pain is a response telling you something. All currents which have a lower frequency than your frequency create blockages when they are not released. Disharmony arises when negative feelings are suppressed. Then you are holding on tightly, and your body stores the repressed feelings. Painkillers only help the body to be quiet for a short period of time. Each cell has its own intelligence and stores all the thoughts that you submit.

I watched the words appare on the paper as I wrote, and the truth they revealed sank in deeply. I knew it was like this, my body was my treasure map in life. All the pain that appeared was the expression of what I had suppressed. That is why I am here now; my desire was to be free. My decision to go to the jungle to heal gave the signal to my system that I was ready to listen, then all the pains came to the surface to be released. When the thoughts of fleeing to get painkillers arose, I knew at the same time that it was nonsense. Part of me wanted to go away, while something deeper held me back here. Looking at it from this angle I was grateful that they came to the surface, which perhaps meant that it was these blockages which now would be released. I kept quiet contemplating the words showing up in front of me. Eventually more people came, some to have a morning dip in the pond, and we chatted until it was time for medicine and breakfast.

The Lanterns Leading the Way

The massage we received wasn't exactly like the one I was used to, here they used a paste made of ginger and I was kneaded from head to toe. The abdominal region received an extra intense innings during which the shaman massaged all the intestines. It was painful and left my whole body burning for hours. Most of us had been granted this treatment so the queue was long. When the massage was over, I was left talking to those who were waiting, and the maestro who sealed the contact with my heart came over to have a chat. He wanted to make a request and asked me to translate into English. He began by saying the next three consecutive ceremonies we were going to have were working sessions, the first two had been to get to know the medicine and to lay the foundation for the three following.

He looked at me and said: "I know you are not afraid, but there are a lot of people here who are, I want you to tell them that we are now going to guide you through a tunnel, but we will light up the way for you with our lanterns, you just have to follow the lights and you are going to get through safely." I just looked at him with a stunned gaze recalling my dream. He had used those same words as the man in the robe had, and there were five of them too. Again, the strong feeling that everything was staged before I came into this life came alive. No wonder I kept having a lot of memories popping up, memories that came roaming in and disappeared. The veil I had seen in another dream, the curtains waving in the wind and letting the background emerge in glimpses, gave me a picture of this without my fully understanding what the dream was trying to show me. The sight greeting me at the end of the tunnel appeared in my memory, whatever was coming I was going to make it. The surroundings and the feeling when I lay in the crystal-clear water were worth more than any challenges. Strengthened by the visions in the dream, I had the advantage of knowing what was to come, I was not afraid.

The day passed at a slow pace; it felt like an aura of something in store which was circling all over the area. The pain changed to a slight discomfort making it possible for me to take a nap in the afternoon. It was going to be a long night, so it was important to be rested. I lay in bed and looked out on a piece of the sky where I captured a condor flying in circles. It felt as if it wanted to give me a message as it flew in circles inside the small open spot in the wall, where I could follow. It was as if it said to me; use your eagle eye, see the bigger picture. I sent a thought of gratitude towards it and fell asleep peacefully. When I woke up there was just time to have a drink before I had to begin fasting for the evening's session. There was a heaviness in my stomach which I hadn't felt before the other ceremonies, a seriousness that penetrated. I wondered what the evening would bring. Although I was excited and a little uneasy, I was also looking forward to it. After the experience in 1991 all fears had disappeared, and I couldn't recall having felt fear since. Well, fear of the postman I had certainly known many times, the bills he put in the mailbox were always a challenge.

Tonight's preparations were the same as the previous one. During the yoga practices I had lain on the mattress and meditated while listening to the beautiful mantras the girl put on the speaker, even with less pain I was not able to do any challenging movements. It was lovely to have this time of concentration and relaxation, and the sounds of the jungle mingled with the music fluttering around. My gaze rested upwards, there was something there that made me feel at home. Maybe it was the symmetry or the living material, or maybe the energy of many previous ceremonies? It was like lying safely in a cocoon, reinforced by the darkness that swept itself around us, becoming denser as the evening sank in, two lanterns lit up the surroundings just enough so that I could get a glimpse of the people around me. After yoga, all sounds, except those coming from the jungle, quieted down. We all waited for the shamans to arrive, and a heavy seriousness felt like a veil around the room, the energy was dense, as if I could have cut through it with a knife. I was excited about what would show up, and I felt something move in my stomach region. Finally, I could hear the maestros walking towards us chatting and laughing. Now it starts, I thought, the wait is over.

The Anaconda

The shamans finished their ritual whilst chatting and laughing. It was good to see the calm and confidence they were radiating, it rubbed off any anxiety and I felt that they always knew what they were doing. The medicine hadn't been as bad as everyone had said, but tonight I understood what they meant, it was *awful*. I had to hurry back to the mattress and light a mapacho so as not to vomit right away. Mapacho is a sacred tobacco for the shamans, and it is used to protect them against evil forces. It is a very strong medicine and should not be inhaled, it is only to be blown out into the air or towards the body to cleanse it. It helped me to change the taste and I felt my stomach calm down. I took a deep breath and concentrated on what was going on around me to help shift my focus, and my stomach calmed down even more. A tension had come in after the ayahuasca had been ingested, something that I hadn't felt in the same way previously. There was something different, and the shamans' words echoed in my head; it was time to go into the tunnel.

As they turned off the lights I kept my focus on my breathing, but I could feel the energy change in the room, not only the seriousness which I had felt build up during the day, I could also feel fear seeping into this electrical atmosphere. No one said anything and I heard the maestros blowing out the mapacho from time to time, which I could smell coming around me, swaddling itself around as an invisible cloak. It made me feel safe and seen, I was not alone. The dream I had had at home also helped to give me peace of mind, although I noticed how one thought after another tried to capture my attention. I managed to let them pass by. The silence can be an ordeal sometimes, and this evening I thought that it lasted for a very long time. After a while I felt the snake begin to awaken in my abdominal region. The spirit of ayahuasca is the anaconda, and many have seen it meandering around the room or around themselves while they were working with the medicine.

The designs of the medicine began to unfold in beautiful colours and patterns, they flickered by so quickly that I couldn't catch them. I wanted to memorise everything so that I could draw them afterwards, but it was like my brain wasn't allowed to keep the pictures. I just had to breathed in and surrendered to whatever came. It felt like I could not only see the geometry, but as if they were also penetrating the cells throughout my body. It reminded me a bit of the experience I had had when I was lying in bed with the love washing through me, it came with a buzzing sound that vibrated throughout my whole body. It had taken a long time to penetrate the cells and open them up and clean all the old energies back then. The exact same feeling was what I could feel in my body now.

I relaxed as I enjoyed the scenario behind my closed eyes, what was going on in my body, I left to itself. After a while it was as if I hit a wall and all became dark, the picture changed, and I could see myself running up the green hill towards the southern house. This time there were several children present, but I wanted to play by myself next to the stairs. The snake started to move around in my abdominal region and the uneasiness ached. The nausea intencified as the snake circulated around the intestines, I felt how it snatched something here and there before it continued. It lasted for quite a while before it eventually ended up in my stomach where it left the waste products. The nausea became acutely worse, and I began to vomit.

When the first cleansing was over, completely different images started to arise, I saw myself being brought into this world and put in a crib. I cried and moved my arms and legs frenetically while I both saw this baby and I was her at the same time. My mother's thoughts came in clearly as if she were sitting talking directly to me. She didn't realise that I could hear what she was thinking, so she just let them out without filtering. The maestra sitting in front of me started to sing so lovingly my tears began to spurt. I heard her sing: "cry no more little baby, everything is good now," again and again. The scenarios continued while she sang, the movies rolled, and I saw myself growing up while the thoughts my mother sent out were clear as printed ink in a newspaper. Nothing was hidden, it was just an illusion which she surrounded herself with. I got the feeling of an ostrich hiding its head in the sand, thinking no one could see it. When I got to the age of two, I said it was enough, I didn't want to see this anymore. I could see clearly that my mother was in her own pain, so it was okay to send her forgiveness. The song was so filled with love that I just surrendered to it. It was like lying in a warm, loving embrace after having been out in a storm, and I allowed it to soothe me. As she moved on to the next person, I sank heavily back into the chair, tired as after a long day's work.

It wasn't long before I felt the anaconda begin to rumble again, but this time I didn't get pictures of what it cleansed, everything was completely dark. I understood it was about the abuse and was grateful for not having to see it. For the rest of the evening, I was helped to clean up a lot of turmoil and I picked up a lot of phrases that were pronounced in Spanish. When they came out so clearly it was as if I was told they were for me. He or she who sang could be on the other side of the room and the cacophony of voices was like a jumble of sounds. Each icaro sung directly to me was filled with so much love that I just melted into it, tears kept flowing, but it only did me good. The elder padded my head when he finished and said, "ay ay, gitana," (gypsy). I had to smile, and I thought of the wonderful pictures I had experienced in the last ceremony.

When the evening's work was finished, I fell onto the mattress totally wornout, how was it possible to get so tired. An hour passed before I was able to gather enough strength to go to the bathroom, even though I felt that there was something to be cleansed out, leftovers from the snake. The songs afterwards accompanied by the guitar were like balm for my battered system. These sessions were hard work. Suddenly I heard thunderstorms in the distance, and lightning lit up the sky regularly. Nature is cleaning up for us, I thought, grateful to lie dry with these beautiful lullabies around me. That night I couldn't bear to go back to my cabin, I was too exhausted. I stayed where I was listening to the rain trickle and flow. I didn't wake up until it was light outside, and only one other person was still on his mattress, the rest had gone to their own cabins. I gathered my things and gently staggered home. It was still wet after the downpour of the night, and I sucked in the pure sweet scent of the flowers along the path.

I picked up a cup of tea on the way back and sat down to document some of the night's devotions. The fact that my mother was distanced wasn't new to me, but to hear the thoughts coming out of her surprised me. I began to understand why I had blocked out all memories of my childhood, several pieces began to fit together in my understanding of myself. Now I could better understand where my perception of the world came from, my insecurities, and how all experiences coloured my way of interacting with those around me. No wonder I had grown up with a feeling of being outside the family, like the black sheep in the flock. The hours flew by quickly as I wrote or sat in contemplation of all that had been shown to me, I almost didn't have time to take a shower before the massage and morning supplement of plants. After a light breakfast several of us gathered around the pond to discuss the night's events. A small shed sold refreshing coconuts; it was like a little oasis of peace around me amid all the chaos inside.

The Aroma of Love

I went to the next night's ceremony with optimism and great courage. It couldn't be any worse than last night, I thought, and I was excited about what was to come. The medicine was, if possible, even harder to swallow and I sat back on the mattress holding my breath and lighting the mapacho as soon as I could. Then I concentrated on breathing calmly to turn the focus outward, I could hear someone vomiting at once, so I wasn't the only one struggling. Imagine choosing this voluntarily! I had to laugh to myself at the thought of what I was exposing myself to. The medicine opened the visions the moment they started singing and I felt the strong smell of mapacho oozing around my body, the colours and surroundings I was looking into were so beautiful, it was easy to slip into this river of energy. I was resentful when a wall of red energy suddenly appeared, and everything went black.

The darkness was dense, and I waited to see what would turn up, and a feeling of falling came over me as if I were in free fall. It went faster and faster and I felt the fear of not knowing where I was heading creep in. The darkness was total, where was I going? What would happen when I reached the bottom? Would I crash-land? My mind was a jumble as I felt the air pressure like a maelstrom. How far was I really going? It didn't end. As soon as this thought emerged, I knew it was up to me to stop the fall, I had the control and the power to end it. Stop, I exclaimed in my mind, and all became silent. Where am I now? I tried to look around, but it was completely dark and quiet, so all my senses were eager to figure out what this was.

Icaros started to penetrate the wall of darkness and I remembered the words of those from the dream, and from the maestro: "just follow our lanterns, we will guide you through," I shifted my focus and started listening to the songs. A line came flying towards me; "ayahuasca, do your job, let memories come back." I felt the snake begin to crawl in my abdomen, while memories began to seep into my consciousness, memories of beatings and punishments, all the horrors I had felt every time I did something my father didn't like. They came back as if I were there. Time didn't exist. The snake rumbled and snatched the poison left in my body while I let grief and despair surface. It moved down my legs and I wondered what was hiding there.

The answer came sailing in the moment that I started wondering; it was every word I had swallowed down, all the times I had cried and had been told to stop or else I would get something to cry for. The tears flowed freely while the ayahuasca cleansed. I, who thought I wasn't afraid of anything, now I saw the fear I had had for life itself; it wasn't safe to say anything or to be me. No wonder life had been so extremely difficult, my subconscious told me that I was best off when I was invisible. It was a relief when one of the maestras came and sang her icaro into all this pain, threads of gold were woven in and gathered up the parts of me which I had pushed away. I bathed in the loving atmosphere which the maestra created, while the memories were permitted to be there. Suddenly I felt a heavenly scent pouring out of the maestra, and I inhaled with long breaths, I didn't want to lose a second of this magical aroma. This is the scent of love, I thought, this is how it smells. It was breathtakingly beautiful, and I sucked it in covetously like someone who had been dried out for a long time and who finally got to drink.

For the rest of the evening, it was as if the energetic part of me was being worked on. Pain and fear had created many deposits, and I felt twitches and tremors vibrate in different parts of my body. It meandered and writhed, shook, and trembled, and my spine cracked several times. I understood that the spine was life's support beam, and it had become very kinked. When the ceremony was over it felt like I had a new body. There was a lightness present that I hadn't felt for as long as I could remember, and I could turn my head to either side so far that I could see behind my shoulders. It was as if my whole body was made of jelly as I curled down onto the mattress, now I could rest and listen to the beautiful songs always following. What a work they do, I thought, so tired I couldn't bear to lift a finger. I fell asleep in an instant when I returned to my cabin and slept for so long that I almost lost my morning massage. I hadn't been able to sleep for as long as that since I had arrived, and I was still tired. After the flower bath I went back and fell into a sound sleep again. One work session left, I thought, when I woke up, I would have given a lot, to be able to sleep until the next day. After everything I had gone through, I couldn't believe anything could be left behind.

Since I was so tired, I managed to fall asleep before the icaros started, fortunately the song woke me up. I didn't have the strength to fight anything, and I let all experiences come and go as they pleased. Every time they sang directly to me, I could feel electrical impulses shoot into my heart, it was as if the dna itself was being renewed. No visions or memories came in that night except for the southern house and the gypsy camp, but there was no doubt that the medicine was working on my energy body. Various scents, some from flowers and others more like sandalwood, came and went as they sang. It was a relief to have a ceremony where I got to be in a loving atmosphere more than in painful experiences and memories.

When the evening was over, I wanted to sit down on the bench by the pond to enjoy the stars and the relaxed state I was in. On the way down I managed to go over on my ankle, and I heard the tendons creak in protest as I fell in slow motion. Several people came rushing, but I had to get back to myself before I was able to answer them. The assistant came and helped me to get back to the cabin. I was really annoyed with myself. This wasn't an environment in which it was easy to move, so how was I going to get to all the gatherings, the dining hall, and stroll around to admire nature? I imagined that this could take weeks.

The next day I was given an intensely painful massage to get my tendons in place, and a bandage was lashed tightly around my ankle. One of the co-participants provided me with a cane which I could use as a stick, so I limped around as best I could. Before going to bed that evening, I had a special paste smeared around my ankle by the maestro, a paste which he had made for cases such as mine. In the middle of the night, I woke up because darts were shooting up my calf and I felt the energy circulating around the injury. Suddenly there was a shock and movements which were like those which I had experienced during the fall. It was as if the shock in my body was released, and I lay amazed feeling all these sensations going on. Afterwards it was easier to move my foot, so some healing had taken place. I was impressed by their knowledge about nature's plants, and how they can specifically help us. When I got up the next day, I could even walk with a little weight on my foot. I had been anxious about the walk down to the boat as we were going back home in a few days, but with such treatment it would not be a problem.

For the rest of my stay, I was able to relax more. I had let go of the tensions I had been feeling during the first few days and the pain was gone. Now I was a little handicapped due to my ankle, which came as an extra reminder to take life easy. One of the participants told me that what had happened was a warning, someone would break my fall when I got home, but it was a good sign that the treatment that I had received had such a good effect. That's exactly what happened when I was home, and all went well. My sensitivity doubled after my stay in the jungle, and I quickly understood what was evolving. The day we left I could walk normally, even though my ankle was still tender. It was a new person who arrived at Iquitos. It was as if life had become more colourful, as if the light streaming towards me was ridden of the murky stuff and now, I could see more clearly.

I was full of gratitude; the trip had been more healing than I could ever have imagined. The environment had been totally unknown to me, but I had felt at home immediately. It was almost as if I had been longing to be there without realising that, and it had given me more than I could have hoped for. Now I went home with a singing heart, ready to embark on the life that was about to unfold. Ayahuasca had done her job, so I didn't need any more from her. Haha, how wrong I was. She had called me, and I was delighted that I had followed her voice, but I didn't know that she had more up her sleeve. Right now, I wanted to use the time to integrate all the events I had experienced and my newly acquired discoveries.

Dance of the Soul

The first week at home I was in bed with a high fever. I wasn't sick with flu or anything, except for the temperature that was ravaging my body. After the demanding work I had been through it was perfectly fine to do nothing, to just lie in bed and sleep. It was like my body wanted to burn up the slag, the leftovers from the energetic replacement. Even this couldn't put a damper on the calm and lightness I experienced. It was like a new song had taken root in my heart, and I just wanted to smile at the world. However, as my new friend from the jungle had predicted, there was somebody that I discovered who didn't want me to be well. My reinforced intuition made me aware of this before it escalated, and once it was sorted out, I could sit down and go through the events from the last few months. I often sat out in the garden writing on my laptop. The roses were now in full bloom and the garden was at its best. There was much to think about and a new idea of how identity is created came into my awareness. This clarity made it so much easier to see myself from the outside, and a new perspective could emerge. The subconscious that had coloured my perception of the world was the basis of my thoughts, and now I had access to a lot of what it contained. The plants and the scents from them accompanied the words floating through.

It is the shadows that shape the soul. When we are inside the darkness everything seems dark, and when we are in the light everything seems bright. By going through the darkness of suffering we shade ourselves so that we can become visible to ourselves. It gives us depth, and we learn empathy when we have learned to know the pain. Light is wisdom, and darkness is absence of knowledge. When we are in the absence of light, we do not know what is around us. We do not even know there is anything more to glimpse. The absence of light hides the recollection of who we are and where we come from, and we blame the pain on the outside, onto others. We blame the world. We blame others or put blame onto circumstances, without understanding where it comes from. When we blame others, we are also giving our power away. We become victims of something which we cannot control or change. By letting go of being a victim we will find our way back to ourselves, and we will take back our own power. Then we give the soul its new substance. To find our way back we must release the layers of protection around the heart. We must dare to be vulnerable, to let others see how we feel. This is also the first test in courage, because it takes courage to let the vulnerability come forward. This is the first step into love. The heart is the point of contact into the soul, to the light and the memory of who you are.

Everything was self-evident when I read the words that had come to me. Why hadn't I seen this earlier? It had been many years since I had forgiven my grandfather and put my experiences behind me, so what had been holding me back? Much that I didn't know had come to light, and the pain my parents had acted from had become visible to me. This had made it easy to forgive. I also knew that forgiveness wasn't about saying that what had occurred to me was okay, it was an act where I freed myself from ancient history. I put down the weight those experiences had given me and what I had been carrying. It was more a decision to no longer bring my past into the future.

Forgiveness is a conscious choice to let go and release the pain and this is what loosens me from the history that lives in time. When I thought about the dream which showed me the creation of time, I now could understand why it had been shown to me. By releasing the yoke that had hung there, it became possible for me to live in the now. For as long as I was chained to a previous event, I was being dragged backwards again and again. The chains were like tentacles holding me tight, as if they were giving permission to the spider to spin its web around me. When I chose to put down everything that had given rise to the pain, I was free. By doing this, I was also letting others have room to sort things out for themselves and their own consciences. When I disentangled myself, I was no longer entangled in any circumstances from outside, and I could let it be between them and God. The more I became aware of what had bound me, the easier it became to be in the now. In glimpses, the space between the thoughts became clearer.

Although more revelations and insights were becoming clear to me, I also felt that there was something I couldn't get hold of. I knew that I was on the right track, but I wanted to go back to the love I had felt, the vision of the power rushing out of me and everything that had happened afterwards. I had to get hold of this at whatever cost. The truth was going to come out, and I knew that I wasn't there yet, there was more. I spent the summer writing, meditating, and reading books. What I had seen in the ceremonies had opened my perception to a reality which had been unknown to me. When I was in the visions, they felt more real than my everyday consciousness, they were like the dreams I had on a regular basis. When I was asleep my beliefs and thoughts were not present, and then I could reach into parts of consciousness that were hidden to me during my waking hours. In that state my subconscious could show me what I couldn't see when I was awake, and the insights that came through my lucid dreams stuck like nails into my mind. They could suddenly appear in my mind and give of their wisdom layer by layer many years after they had shown up the first time. After I had signed up for the retreat in the jungle I could easily get into the same state even when meditating. Here I could ask questions and the answers I got often surprised me.

One afternoon as I sat down writing and struggling to find the words, I decided to ask for help from my guides. I put my lap-top away, leaned back, closed my eyes, and prayed that the words would shuffle in the right way so that what I wanted to express could be understandable. After a few moments of concentrating on my breathing, a scenario began to play behind my closed eyes. I saw Snow White lying in the basket, while the queen walked over to the mirror: "Mirror, mirror on the wall, who is most beautiful in the world?" The queen looked at herself as the mirror replied: "You, my queen, are the most beautiful here." She was content and moved on until the next time she needed confirmation. This time, she got a completely different answer, and she became furious, Snow White was now the most beautiful in the world and that was not acceptable. She picked up a basket into which she put the little baby and went deep into the forest where she put down the basket and left, and we all know how that went.

As I watched the film unfold the understanding came by itself at the same time, and I understood that we have both the queen and Snow White inside us. The struggle arises when we come into conflict with the demands of the world. We learn to behave in the ways expected of us, and eventually the mirror becomes more important than our inner voice. Our true selves are hidden by the defences which we build up and which we then hide behind. Every time the inner voice tries to come forward, we are quick to put it back to sleep again. We try to kill it, but it cannot die. The seven dwarves I saw as small nature spirits who look after us and guide us on the journey of life. It was also no coincidence that there were seven dwarves. This number is often repeated in the scriptures as a sacred symbol; the bible says the seventh day will be the day of rest and should be kept holy, the rainbow has seven colours that harmonise with the seven main chakras in the body. Chakras are energy wheels that control the exchange between energy in and energy out. I was surprised by this scenario, it wasn't what I had expected, but it made sense. The queen was an image of the ego, the part that needs the mirror to affirm itself. When the feedback is negative, it gets fearful. There may be fear from the ego of not being good enough or of not being loved, which in turn leads to the perception of an unsafe world. To compensate for insecurity or fear, we begin to control our surroundings. Snow White grew up in innocence, happy only by caring for those who looked after her. This, I understood, came directly from the love we are. It just wants to give and doesn't worry if it is good enough.

The mechanism that had been controlling me my whole life became increasingly visible. No wonder I had attracted men who affirmed my thoughts of not being good enough. If I had put a piece of apple in little Snow White's throat, I had to be the one removing it. Now I completely understood why the words were stuck in my throat. The love I had experienced during icaros, the scents they emitted when they sang, made the little girl open her eyes in amazement. I tried to tell my family about what I was experiencing, but each time they just looked at me as if I was weird.

After a strange event, where I experienced everything that I now saw and understood disappeared, I realised how weird my experiences could sound. It was as if the filter had returned and shadowed the inner senses again, the layers that had been removed when the love flowed through me the first time, in 1991, and with the help from the shamans. For two hours, the world on the outside was the only real one, and I wondered for a moment if all my experiences were fake. This left me with a deep understanding of those who didn't get what I was trying to express. When the world is the only reality that is, what I talked about would seem like a fantasy world, a fairy tale. This experience made me more careful about what I told and to whom. Luckily, I had a couple of girlfriends with whom I could share, and

I found a lot of like-minded people on youtube I could listen to, I needed to hear others with similar experiences. The thought that it was me who was starting to get crazy sometimes came creeping in after this event, so it was necessary to listen to other people's supernatural stories. Nothing was going to stop my curiosity and exploration, and I felt strongly that I was guided.

The isolation I chose was necessary as I lured little Snow White out of the woods. Several memories of my childhood surfaced, happy episodes where I jumped and bounced, climbed trees, or sat quietly playing with dolls in the garden. There were a lot of kids in the street where we lived, and we always found something to do. I remembered how we hit the ball against the wall, had cycling competitions arranged by my brother, and several other games where all the children in the street played together, the camaraderie between us children was strong, so that side of my childhood was the best. A book I was very fond of did suddenly pop into my memory, it was called "The House of Sjongfalleri." It was a story about little trolls who built houses using sheets of music. I remembered how I read it every night and sang while I was in this merry union with them until the book disintegrated. I have tried to find the book again, but without any luck so far.

I was happy to restore some of the memories from these early years, and it dawned on me that by displacing what was painful and difficult, the good memories had also been lost. Now I can remember trips we took with tents and fishing rods and skiing on the high mountain with cocoa and near and dear friends. The shamans had cleansed the chaos and consequently more colours and shades came in from my life. Even though my parents had their challenges, I knew they were doing what they thought was right. On one occasion my father told me that their conviction had been that babies came in as empty shells, and that they were raised as respectable adults through the setting of boundaries. He added: "how on earth could we think anything like that" while he fell silent and looked down. In the past he had also bragged about how obedient we were. He used to tell how the other parents wanted to know how to have children who were so kind. Now he added, "I wonder why," and became quiet and thoughtful. I knew I had chosen them as my parents so I could no longer blame them for my difficult life.

The whole summer I was writing down insights and experiences unfolding after coming home. The dream I had had as a little girl began to appear in my memory again. I saw the huge black spider in front of me, and how, full of horror, I pressed myself against the brick wall. There was no one to save me, something I knew with unfailing certainty. Now there was a new layer of understanding. I understood that this was the time when fear took hold and held me captive in its web of lies. Only I could untangle myself from this, no one could come and rescue me from the cocoon that was spun around me. I was the one who believed this to be true. This was the time I was consumed in the matrix, and only I could dissolve the grip of the spider's net holding me tight.

Although I had stopped being afraid of death in 1991, my fear of life was great. I realised that this had created my escape away from myself, for as long as I saw the world as a dangerous place, I refused to let my soul be present in my body, just like Snow White living deep in the woods, beyond the hustle and bustle of the world. In the same way I had been hiding, but I was somewhere in there. I had to be who I was any moment until I could bring all of her out front, just like the angels who held my heart together. The love that had woken me up was guiding me always, and my smile unfolded as my new perspective in which I was looking from, changed my worldview.

My view of what life consisted of was in constant expansion. I went from a belief that the world ruled me, to my having the power to create the world I was living in. The feeling of freedom took over by shifting the focus from being a victim of circumstances to being the creator of it, and the power in me came to light. I felt a new awakening as if feeding myself into myself. The surrounding nature became alive, it spoke to me, and I opened my eyes so that I could see how beautiful it was. I began to enjoy being present in my body here and now. My senses came to life, and the more I allowed them to be, the clearer my inner senses became. Now I understood the people who had told me that I needed grounding, which I had never quite understood. It was okay for me to imagine a thread that would go from me into the middle of the earth, but I had never quite understood what it really meant until now. To be grounded simply means to be fully present here, in this life. If I fled in terror, I wouldn't be fully present in my body. This body was given to me as a gift by mother earth so that my soul could travel in the physical realm. It was supposed to experience feelings and to teach me to make the right choices. Then I had to be in it.

I was ecstatic about everything that arose from somewhere deep inside of me. The clearer I became to myself the more was opened. It was like a journey of discovery where the magic became visible, the door that was closed in my childhood was about to open wide. I started noticing all the synchronous events. Every time I had a question, the answer magically popped up right away, either by books presented to me, other people, or incidents occurring. Time ceased to exist as before, and I thought of the dream which had shown me how time was created. I understood that what I was experiencing existed outside of time and beyond words. There would be sudden downloads while walking outside in nature, but when I got home and tried to write them down on paper, it was like they dissolved. It was like getting a huge ball of knowledge which I was supposed to take with me into time, I had to stretch out in a line what was all entangled and connected and convey it with an understandable language. Every time I tried, the words shuffled, and I was left tearing my hair in frustration. It was as if the words cut the understanding into pieces, and all became disconnected.

How was I going to express in words what I saw and understood? I wrote and rewrote and wrote again, I just had to get it down, afraid that it would be gone from my memory. There were many pages where I said the same thing in different ways, and my closest friends had to listen to my fumbling explanations in search for the right words to describe it. I needed someone outside of myself to check if they understood what I tried to convey. On my inside I had no doubts, but I needed feedback on how it was perceived when I communicated it out to the world. Did they understand what I meant, or did I have to explain it in another way? Maybe it wasn't so easy to convey something I barely understood myself, what came needed a while to be processed in the brain. For the most part what came in through downloads lay outside of the normal way of thinking and I had to digest and contemplate before I accepted anything. What felt right needed some time to be expressed in words.

A Universal Design

When autumn arrived, a friend asked if I wanted to join the Santo Daime Church. I had read about it but wasn't sure if it was for me. After some back and forth I decided to join her. I had no idea what it would be like as the whole setup was arranged in a completely different way. I thought it might be interesting to try though. I googled and found out the church started in Brazil in the 1930s by a poor guy who went into the jungle in search of work. He could neither read nor write, and the village where he lived was one of the poorest, they all lived under hard conditions, and it was difficult to maintain the needs of daily life without an income. He eventually decided to leave the village hoping to find something to do somewhere else. When he returned after a long time, his family was sure he was dead. It turned out that he had run into shamans who introduced him to ayahuasca. During the ceremonies he had had countless visions where he was taught how to form a church and use the hymns that he downloaded during ceremonies. These songs were the start of what is now the Santo Daime church which has spread around the world over the last decades. The liturgy they use comes from the Catholic set-up which was what he had learned growing up. The entire ceremony takes place in the light, unlike the shamans who work in darkness, and they dance or sit whilst the hymns are sung.

The church they often used on the site we traveled to was a stately building from the late 1800s built with bricks. The windows were original and showed beautiful colourful mosaic images depicting stories from the bible. The church was located outside the city, and it was surrounded by a beautiful park where we could see a graveyard surrounding the building. I could see many old gravestones between the big trees. We were surprised by the amount of people showing up, there were probably two hundred, and many of them were busy arranging the setup. It felt like coming into a lively city hall filled with loving energies. The room was large and airy and the dome in the ceiling was incredibly beautiful with its old mosaic windows. People greeted us with a smile, and we were asked where we came from, and they welcomed us. They informed us how it was all going to be, and we stood in the middle of all activities and smiled at the mood of hospitality and equality. It was heartwarming and I felt my shoulders slump. I could hear no superficial chatter, which has never been my favourite, and when someone asked a question, they listened to the answer.

Since this was supposed to be a healing gathering (cura), we sat on chairs. They were placed in a hexagon, three sides with the women and three with the men and in the middle, there was a beautifully decorated altar where the musicians gathered with their instruments. One person was playing the accordion, another a guitar, one was playing drums, and the last was playing a flute. In addition, many people had maracas. This was very different from what I had experienced, so I was excited to see how the work would be. There was no place to hide away in the darkness, and I thought of all the times my arms and legs had lived their own lives under the influence of the medicine. I had to let everything be as it would be and hope for the best. When the music started, I was surprised at how wonderful it sounded, and I let myself be carried away by the melody and rhythm. Everyone was singing and it gave a richness to the music that was magical, it was like being in the middle of a wave of a heavenly choir.

I closed my eyes and let myself go where the wave led me. The less resistance the easier it is for the medicine to do its work; this I had learned. Tones from the accordion began to come through strongly, and I was pushed upwards in a golden spiral. I ended up on something resembling a mountaintop and was looking down on what was happening beneath me. There I was shown how the tones penetrated a layer to enter an aspect of the soul hidden behind as if it were lying in a cave. I could see clearly that when the tone found such a cave, it was as if the vibration from the tone penetrated through it, and the part that was hiding in darkness found its way back to the light, to connect with the soul. The observation was so interesting that I forgot everything else. Eventually, the songs came back into focus, and the lyrics penetrated my consciousness. All the songs are in Portuguese, but since I know Spanish, I understood most of the words, I kept singing along until the next medicine was served. A gathering with the Santo Daime congregation can last anywhere from six to ten hours, and there are several servings. Later in the evening I got a vision that has subsequently come up on a regular basis, and each time it has shown me new layers of understanding.

A white fog appears in front of me while at the same time I get the feeling of whirling back and forth at a fast pace. I look at it and wonder what it is. The speed slows down and I catch a glimpse of something that makes me focus consciously. The swirling stops completely and now I can see the impenetrable grey-white cloud made of fog-like spirals standing on a high edge, they look like the photos NASA puts out of nebulas. Between these spirals I can see Jesus and Mary, and they look directly at me. I notice that they are standing on the other side of these fog clouds, and where they are there is only green grass and flowers. There is nothing that hides the view where they are standing, I know they can see me all the time, that they are not limited by the fog that is blocking my vision. In the second that our eyes meet, I know they have always followed me. Even though I lost sight of them, they haven't lost touch with me. I want to cross over to where they are standing, but it is as if an invisible wall obstructs the passage. I am standing completely still without any thoughts being able to enter, and I cannot get enough of what they radiate. No words are conveyed, but the energy contains everything that I need to know. The vision dissolves and I become conscious of my body again as the song and text penetrates my mind and brings me back into focus, into the here and now.

After the ceremony finished, food and fruit were served while we walked around chatting and laughing. I saw the accordion player, and on a whim, I went over to tell her what I had seen and to thank her for the work I saw she was doing. When I finished, she looked at me for a long time with tears in her eyes before she replied: "I have been wondering lately if I am really making a difference with my playing, I was considering whether to put the accordion away." My heart grew soft and warm as she spoke, and I understood why this vision had been shown to me; it came to be shared. We chatted for a long time, a warm conversation with a soulmate. I am constantly amazed by the design of the universe, the more I opened my vision the clearer it became how I was guided all the way to find the truth I was searching for.

When I got home, I wondered what the vision of the fog clouds meant, but it took a couple of years before it suddenly reappeared one day as I was writing, and this time I got an explanation of what it was; the nebulas were resembling my thoughts! In an instant I knew that if I jumped from one thought to the next, there was no way to see in between all the words occupying my mind. I saw that by being drawn into a thought it pulled me into the spiral of the story it wanted to tell. This story was limited, so when it finished, I jumped on to a new thought, then to the next one. Each time the thought completed its story the next one appeared, and in the end, I just returned to the beginning. This was the swirling back and forth. When all I did was to go into different thought patterns, I lost the space in between them. Eckart Tolle talks about this in his books, and now I clearly understand what he meant. We must find the silence; it is in the space between the words or thoughts, we could find reality. The thoughts were the fog creating what we believed to be true, when we quiet down the mind the reality would show itself. It was so obvious that I couldn't understand how I hadn't seen this before. It is all in front of us, we only need to open our eyes and not listen to the mind all the time.

I was almost overwhelmed by what I had been shown in the vision. What happened when I fell silent and could see between the layers, was Jesus and Mary. I thought about the experience that came the night after being washed by God's energy, when I asked Jesus if he was involved in what happened to me. Then, as I mentioned, I had ended up in an ecstasy of joy, a drunkenness from the energies pouring through me. I told my parents what had happened to me at the time and was met with opposition when God and Jesus were mentioned. They had never submitted to any faith, even though we were sent to Sunday school every week. One of my grandmothers, my dad's mum, was a deep believer, reading the bible every day. She never talked about her beliefs, but I think that she needed comfort in her harsh life. She was a psychic, as many of my aunts and cousins are as well, a topic we couldn't talk about as though it would be shameful to see something others could not. The coffee grounds became the means they used to share what they saw, which made me start to drink coffee every summer from the age of fourteen. I remember thinking it tasted awful, but if I wanted my grandmother to look into the cup, I had to drink the coffee myself.

My other grandmother grew up in a Laestadian environment, a cult with rigid beliefs where everything was sinful. They had no curtains in the windows, flowers inside or radios, and all play was strictly forbidden on Sundays, that was the day of prayers and contemplation.

Women were not allowed to speak in congregations, and they were subject to men's laws and regulations. Although my grandparents moved from there, the upbringing my mother received was coloured by my grandmother's experiences. My mother once told me about how scared she had been when they were dragged to meetings and people spoke in tongues, and this caused her to shun everything that had to do with religion. A little strange that we were sent to Sunday school, but it was probably so that my parents could get some much-needed free time. When I tried to find answers with religious believers, I also did not find what I was looking for, and accepted that I had to find them elsewhere. I really wondered where Jesus came into the picture. He was kind of a property of the church, and I didn't want to go there. Mother Mary was the one I related to, and I felt a deep relationship with her. She sometimes came to me in my dreams, and I had several experiences where I could feel her presence. In one of the dreams, I was in a large and neat area, where there were many souls.

I become aware that I am in the middle of a bustling life with many souls and a lot of activity. I am heading towards a gate at the end of the plaza, and I walk with determination as if I know where I am going. I open the gate and walk through. When I close the gate behind me a silence radiates in the whole area, it is a completely different atmosphere here. The hectic energies outside the gate are replaced with a deep silence and tranquility. It feels as if I have entered a sacred space. I look up to the side and I see Mother Mary standing halfway up the hill. She stands perfectly still and looks out at something. I move towards her as if I am sliding up, and I stop just below where she is standing, slightly to her left. Then I turn to look the same way to see what she is looking at. The whole universe comes into view, and far away I glimpse the physical world. I see how every thought and every soul's intention comes towards me. Everything is visible, even every strand of hair can be seen from here. Now I understand how she can see everything that is going on. She pays attention all the time and cares for everything and everyone. Nothing escapes her gaze.

The dream was a bit diffuse when I woke up, as if I was not allowed to remember everything clearly. I remembered my surprise when I saw our world from that point of view, and I remembered my thoughts while there, but the picture of what I saw was like seeing through frosted glass. What I will never forget is the feeling that I had on waking up; I felt as if I had been on holy ground. The feeling comes back just by writing this. The peace in the area was indescribable and I was full of gratitude for being invited in. It was like being in eternity, just Mary and me and the view of all that is. This vision, as I would rather call it, gave me a special relationship with her. Jesus was with me as a dear brother, but it was her who I related to. After the vision of the space between thoughts returned to my memory, I became more curious about who Jesus really is. I saw myself as spiritual, but not religious, which I still do. Every time I talked to someone who was active in the church, I had to face prejudice and a feeling of banging my head against a brick wall. When I went to gatherings or retreats with like-minded people, it was like entering a family party were love and acceptance was flowing unhindered, and joy and laughter came easily.

Both Buddhism and Hinduism have helped me in the search for truth so why condemn them? Their teachings were all about acceptance and love, and that we should go inside ourselves to look for answers. When I read what Jesus was saying, more than the dogmas taught by the church, I could feel it strengthening something inside me. He kept repeating; "have faith, and it will be given, go into your chamber and make contact with your father, your body is your temple," and the like. My world was meditation and contemplation, the answers came by themselves when I let silence take over. It usually came as a quiet voice, or thought, but sometimes it came like a thunderclap.

The visions were so clear whether they came through dreams or in meditations, so I wrote them down and contemplated, meditated, and asked. My curiosity had no limits, and I wouldn't give up until I had all the answers. Eventually I felt the ayahuasca start to call me again. Does she have more she wants to accomplish, I thought, what could it be this time? During one of the first ceremonies, I had seen how the medicine called in those who are ready, and I understood it was not me who found ayahuasca, it was she who had found me.

Greetings from the Condor

Some days after I felt the pull, I received an email from the place I had been to previously. They said that one of their shamans, a woman who had practiced healing for over fifty years, was now building a retreat center at her home with her family, where they were offering 'dietas'. Her daughters were two of the shamans I had met when I was in the jungle, and she also had a son who walked in her footsteps. The daughters were incredibly warm and loving so I knew that they were genuine in their desire to help, and now they wanted to start their own retreats at their home. During a dieta we drink the essence of the plant we choose, a small glass daily, and we eat a minimal amount of food so that the plant to be the focus in the body. I decided to go and wanted to diet a flower that would help me to get in touch with my creativity and words, and providing increased healing for rheumatic ailments and a deeper contact with dreams. Even though I was almost pain-free, I could still occasionally feel a tenderness in my joints.

A few months later I went for my first dieta. The place they had built was considerably smaller than the other place, with fewer people and a lot of tranquility. They had done a lot to create a safe and practical place to be in, and I quickly felt at home. In the case of going into the dieta, the diet I had to start at home was even stricter than before. The amount we were to consume while dieting the plant is also reduced to a minimum so that the energy in the body is weakened. We were served breakfast and lunch consisting of rice with some vegetables and herbs or a light soup. Mostly I just had lunch since I chose to fast for a few hours after each ceremony. For some it was difficult, they were hungry all the time and wanted more food, I thought it was great to feel light and clean inside. One meal a day gave my system tranquility, and it felt like even the mind couldn't disturb this harmony.

Three trips were made to their center dieting with different plants each time, and I had many strong experiences. The words began to flow more easily as if a barrier had been lifted, and my mind did not have power over me as before. Mother Ynez had so much care for us, I saw her going between the cabins to do tasks for people every day. Where I was the first time, we were not allowed to have contact with the maestros, here everything was open, and we could contact them if we needed to. Maestra came almost every afternoon to check our aura and energy, and to give us a blow of mapacho as an extra protection. I enjoyed every hour, I have never found that energy and atmosphere anywhere else, just thinking of it makes me long to be there again.

The second time I went there, a friend joined me. This time we had to spend the night in Lima to take the morning flight to Pucalpa, last time I had booked the last flight from Lima and had missed it, and I didn't want that to happen again. It had been quite a process to get a new ticket for the next departure, I even had to leave the airport and find someone outside that would sell tickets to me. We therefore chose a small place nearby where we could sleep for a few hours. Early in the morning, it was five o'clock, I woke up and felt wide awake. The room was completely dark, and as we could sleep for another hour, I didn't want to wake up my friend by turning the light on, so I chose to stay in bed. I can use this time to meditate, I thought, so I closed my eyes and in an instant, I was somewhere else. It was so real I could see every detail as clearly as if I am there again.

I see myself opening a large, double door of mahogany, and I look into a beautiful room. It resembles an English library, with heavy chesterfield furniture placed in the middle of the room. A large fireplace adorns the wall directly in front. Big, solid bookshelves fill the walls on both sides, and dense, deep red velour curtains are hanging in front of the windows. Gold-coloured cords, with large tassels, hold them apart to let the light in. It is a great room, and it is familiar. As soon as I open the door, I am left standing paralysed in amazement, in front of me I see huge orbs (globes) floating around in the room, they are in different sizes, and glow in many colours. I open my eyes wide in joy and amazement and call out to my friend.

"Look," I say, as she stands next to me:"we can go inside and feel the energies of the angels if we want, we have just forgotten that we can do this." I am in ecstatic bliss over this surprise, now I remember. The surroundings shift and we are walking outside on a deserted road, no buildings or people are present except for a man who I see walking towards us. He is tall and slender with thick dark hair, and he stops in front of me. We look into each other's eyes for a while, then we continue walking in each direction; "that was the strangest thing ever," I say as we stroll on,"looking into his eyes I saw myself."

It feels like I am waking up and a new scenario appears; a huge sun is shining right in front of where I am standing. It shines with a golden light and I can see without difficulty. Then I am told I will be shown the way I need to go when I am looking for myself. It starts at the bottom, from the point where I am standing, and meanders and swings around the sun in a long and winding road. Slowly I see it turn around the sun on the outside and end up on the top of it before it goes inside and ends. Then I am shown the way I will go to find myself if I search for God. I watch as the line goes from me and directly into the sun, it is no more than a few centimeters long. I stand there looking at what is unfolding, then suddenly I am aware that I am lying in bed again.

It took time before I managed to gather myself, I awakened, and then I awoke again. Where was I? It was still pitch dark, so it wasn't easy to orientate right away, I stayed quiet for a while to reorientate myself into the world I was supposed to be in. Everything had happened so fast, yet it felt like an eternity. There were still five minutes left until the alarm would go off, so I must have been gone for fifty minutes.

As we had our breakfast, I told her what had happened to me, and she smiled, feeling honoured to have been part of my dream. During the first meeting with the shamans, I told them about the experience. Ynez' husband, David, smiled from ear to ear, nodding persistently, signalling that what I had dreamt was true. He is one of the most heartfelt people I have met. He is 'tabacero', that is, he has dieted the mapacho to connect with its spirit, and he diligently blows out the smoke for protection during ceremonies. His first task is to accompany Ynez when she is working, but he also looks after everyone else. I can't count all the times I have felt the smoke from his pipe wrap around me like a cloak. Ynez is a well-known healer in the area, and this has led to her having some enemies. Not everyone is familiar with what she represents, and many feel fear when told that it is about spirit and energies. When she is working, negative energies sometimes try to get a hold of her. Her children are always involved in what is happening around her, and I experienced on one occasion that her son had to interrupt the icaros he was singing and come to her rescue. They see the spirit world and have a very different view of what is going on between heaven and earth than those of us who don't see it. David was left several times sitting in front of me when Ynez moved on, and I could feel the strength of his low humming; something moved deep, deep down every time he was sitting in front of me, like he could see what was there. I don't know what was moving, but it felt like it came from something far away, as a final threshold I had to clear.

On another occasion I saw Ynez approaching me as she sang to those in the circle. When she was singing to my neighbour, it felt as if she was singing to me too. The only thing I saw of her was a luminous sphere, like the sun in the vision, she was covered in a light that was so bright that I fell silent. As she sat in front of me, I felt love floating out along with the song. In gratitude I began to send the love back to her, and it returned to me even more strongly. I kept thinking, she is the one who should have the love for the work she is doing, and the love floated even more strongly back towards me. It was a strong experience, where my heart expanded and became filled with more love every time it returned. Then I understood that to open the heart is not a one-time event, but a continuous process that never ends. My entire chest expanded so much it started to hurt. After this evening I understood that this is what we are doing in this world; we are here to open our hearts more and more. The more I include people or hurts that had occurred to me during my life in this love, the more it would grow inside me, it is like I am in constant expansion. I also understood the only truth there is, is love, the rest is creation in this love.

In two of the ceremonies, I was able to see a group of people, or spirits, who gathered further away from where I was. The surroundings were a plateau with barren vegetation, and the mountains towering upwards, mighty mountains standing like a wreath around. One of the figures broke free from the group and came walking towards me. It was a male energy, but I couldn't see who it was. First, I thought that it was someone walking in front of me in the room where I was sitting, and I didn't take much notice, so he turned around and went back to the others. Then I remembered that the room was dark and that my eyes were closed too, so it couldn't have been someone outside of me. I called him back and he turned and came towards me again. I still couldn't figure out who he was or hear what he tried to say, so after a while he went back to the others again. A couple of months after I returned home, I was learned who it was.

The last retreat I joined, one year before everything was shut down due to the pandemic, I had an incredible experience before the last ceremony. I had collected the things I was going to bring with me to the maloca and walked out of the tambo. It was a small terrain in the back, surrounded by trees and bushes. I looked up at the sky, feeling grateful and honoured to have been gifted one more visit to this place, then I noticed a condor flying high up in the blue sky. I was left standing admiring this great bird as it got closer and closer. Finally, it came sailing all the way down to the ground, next to the cabin, and it flew three laps just above the ground. I was paralysed as it flew straight towards me and over my head, so close that I could have reached out my hand and touched it. I could see every feather, brown ones which formed a beautiful pattern together with the black ones under both wings. It was huge. I saw it fly up, make a turn, and come back. This time it circulated three times over the neighbouring cabin before it flew up again and disappeared. What a magical experience. I was left standing with big eyes and a wide-open mouth for a while, until I managed to tear myself away. Both the person who lived in the neighbouring hut and I had dieted a tree where the condor builds its nest. It felt as though we were blessed, we were seen and recognised by the great bird. It was an incredibly strong end to the last trip I have taken to that place so far, and I went to the ceremony with a big smile on my face and in my heart.

Light as a Feather

The eternal expansion of the heart, the feeling of my entire chest letting in more love when my focus was on giving, had changed something in me, I understood that everything I had forgiven and let go, gave me more room for love to flow through. It was like opening a reservoir that I hadn't known was there. I had experienced God's love, but I didn't know I had to leave behind all the stories to make room for it to flourish. The more I gave, the more I would be given. It was a law of nature I had heard of, but not paid so much attention to. The years I was alone with two small children I had then longed for a partner who could give me love. The insight that I had gained while Ynez was singing, had shown me that I had to start with myself. When looking for love outside myself, thinking that I was lacking, I would create more of what I was lacking. It was when I was in the abundance of love, when I scooped it out, that I would receive more love. Fear and love cannot exist in the same environment at the same time, so it was important to be aware of where I had my focus. I wish I had known this then, but the journey couldn't be any different, this revelation led me to this moment, to get *this* insight.

During my education to be a nurse, continuing studies to be a psychiatric nurse, and then somatic experiencing (trauma techniques), there had been a lot of inner child work. Eventually I realised that when we do this type of work, we are together with the child in the present time. Time only exists in our brain, whilst in fact everything really happens in the moment. It is not easy to grasp from a linear point of view, but the insight I had now made me look at life like a tube. All moments, all experiences, were layer upon layers that lay on top of each other. When we helped the child inside us, we were our own guide, because no one can know the child better than the one who has experienced the episodes. I became in a way my own guardian angel. In one of the first ceremonies, I went up to my higher self. I merged with her, and a review of my life started. Instead of showing me the events, I was shown the guides surrounding me. Then I could see that throughout my life they had been present in my aura as if we were one, and I got to see how they wove the energies more tightly around me when life was at its toughest, as if I was being carried. They guided and comforted me and brought me to where I needed to be or led me towards what was needed at the time.

The love I felt from them was total, and I understood that when life was tough, I couldn't feel their presence. My energy was too low during those periods to be able to take in what they had tried to send to me, but they were a part of me that was there all the time. The years went by until I reached today's age, then I held my body as if it was a coat I had taken off, and I sent love to this body which had lived life in the physical world as best as she could. Then I let go of the body and it melted into the ground and disappeared as if it had never existed. After this revelation I realised how protected I always am, and that I am not just a person, but a whole team. We were so welded together; I couldn't separate them from myself. I remembered how lonely and abandoned I had felt through the years, and now understood that it was because they couldn't reach me through the shield I was hiding behind.

As I unleashed my story, I felt how easy life became. My scepticism for the possibility that good things could happen completely disappeared, now I could wake up in the morning and believe that it would be a nice day. The magic became visible again when I realised that I am the creator of my life, and the anxiety of what life provided me disappeared. I owned the power to create what was coming. My focus was love for life and for myself. Every time that I was in a situation where I had to choose, I went inwards to consult with my intuition, I listened into my heart and waited until I got an answer. The experience with Ynez and the love that only increased the more I gave had left a deep imprint, this was also what I had been shown when I had bathed in the stream of love in 1991. Now I had got confirmation, and I knew that I would never forget, it was imprinted inside me. The love I describe is more than a feeling, it is a vibration, a frequency, the love referred to in the bible, the one that tolerates everything, that doesn't judge, or seek itself. How can it seek what it is? It can only *be* and give from itself. I also knew that I had to live my life, to make the choices I had made to get to where I was now. That is why I was told it was for later in life. It didn't mean I was done with the journey of discovery; this was the start of the most interesting part. I knew that I had reached a point of no return, I had come to a point where I could no longer go back to who I was. Nothing would be as it had been. A new dream appeared after all these conclusions.

I am standing on the edge of a cliff. It is completely flat along the ravine with no vegetation to be seen, only a large, old building at some distance behind me. The wood it was built of was greyish, as if wind and weather had been eating away at it for generations. I look over at the other side where it looks the same way, even the same plateau and the cliff that goes steeply downwards. It is like standing by the cliffs of Grand Canyon and far down I can see the bottom like a narrow strip. A lot of people are busily moving around on the opposite plateau, not so many where I stand, but on the other side it is crowded. I look closely at their movements as they throw themselves off. They try to get enough speed to get over onto my side, up on the plateau where I am standing. There are only a couple of them who make it during the time I am standing there, a lot of them almost get over the edge. I can see they grab with one hand on the edge, losing their grip and rolling back down. Cries of frustration echo around me, over the fact that they didn't make it.

Then, suddenly, I am standing on the other side to throw myself off the cliff too. When it is my turn, I notice that I have a pillow under my arm, I want to put it behind my head. I like to be comfortable, and I think it will be good to rest my head while sliding down the side. My turn comes quickly, and I make myself ready. As soon as I start to slide the thought comes that the pillow might hinder my speed. I want to be fast enough to reach all the way up, so I put it in front of me, on top of my stomach. I hold on tightly while the speed increases, then I understand that it will prevent me from achieving the speed I need if I hold it there too. I know that I must get rid of this pillow completely, I cannot have any baggage. I know that I must be as light as a feather to get all the way up.

I throw it away and feel an instantaneous freedom from everything. The energy now rushing through me is like an ecstasy that doesn't end. Nothing prevents me anymore; I have a lightness that makes me almost jump over the edge and I land with ease on the plateau. Happy and relieved, I get up and brush off the dust, then I turn around and go into the building. A tall and slender lady with blonde hair comes towards me and asks if I want to work there, and my answer is yes. "Then you have to talk to the owner of this company," she says, "only he can teach you and explain the underpinning rules that make this place run." As she speaks, I can feel the energy of the owner coming towards me, it is powerful. Then she guides me to the back of the building and opens the door to one of the rooms. She let me in and tell me to wait. A male figure arrives and begins to explain to me the underlying rules I must follow for this place to exist.

I woke up with a feeling that something new was coming, and I stayed in bed for a while thinking about what the dream had tried to tell me. I recognised the ecstatic freedom, it was the same feeling that washed through me in 1991, and again when I was in the crystal-clear water after coming out of the tunnel. By now I have learned that what I felt came from the frequency of who I am. This is what I am made of and the frequency which I came from, before landing in this harsh environment. To get there I had to get rid of everything; old worn-out thoughts, bad habits, beliefs, all I was holding onto. I was now shown that there was something still lingering, a comfort that was hard to let go of. What could it be, what was the pillow? I knew it was important, that it was necessary to get rid of everything to make it up to where I wanted to be. I couldn't hold on to anything, I had to be light as a feather. Could it be some thoughts or beliefs that still weighed me down? I had to figure it out now that I was made aware that there was something to reveal. These dreams always came with many layers, so I was confident that it would be revealed to me when the time was right.

A New Guide

$\mathbf{B}$y coincidence I got in contact with an older man, a beautiful soul, who was in his eighties. He had started with bio-resonance in his older years and enjoyed helping people in their awakening process. After a friend of mine had an appointment, I became very curious about the work he was doing and felt the familiar pull towards something I had to explore. My friend told me that he talked to the archangels Michael and Raphael, and to other light beings. Jesus was one of his best friends, so this was really someone that I wanted to meet. When we met for the first time, he looked at me knowingly and said he knew that I was coming. I looked at him in amazement and thought about my ninety minute drive; it had felt as if I drove in recollection of something, like a déjà vu.

He measured the imbalances in my body and found microbes and parasites in my brain, there were some bacteria which needed to be cleaned out too. Amongst other things he asked what kind of medicine I had been taking in the jungle, because it hadn't been good for me. I looked at him with wide open eyes and wondered how he knew. I was bitten by spiders every time I was there, and one time my whole arm had swelled. Then I was given medicine made by the maestra from plants she had collected to detoxify the body. The other times I had been bitten she had just smeared something on the bite, but this time I had to drink a glass of the brew she had made. He also asked me if the mosquitos loved me while he put an ampule in the bowl to measure my reaction. I laughed and told him they loved me and apparently so did the spiders. He picked up the ampule and showed me the inscription on it, it said 'mosquitos and spiders'. They are not as fond of me today as they used to be after the treatment, so something did change. I was given charged water I had to drink every day, and I was told to come back when it was empty, which would take a few months.

A few months after the ceremony where I experienced someone in spirit approaching me, it was time to go back to the therapist. "There is someone here who wants to connect with you," I hadn't been there for long when he delivered this message. I looked at him and wondered who it could be. When he began to describe the figure, he saw my eyes became even bigger, the only one who could fit the description was my grandfather, the one who had molested me when I was a child. I told him and he looked directly at me and said, "yes, it is him, he knows what he did and sees it from a completely different angle in the place he is in now. He wants to make amends for the pain he caused you, and he wants to know if he can be a part of your team of guides." I looked up at him, nodded slowly and replied; "that is okay, he is allowed." He almost drilled his eyes into where he saw my grandfather, and warned him pointing with his finger. "You heard what she said, you can go into her team, *but* now you promise to take good care of her." It was said with a voice of thunder, but at the same time as gentle as a breeze. He fell silent and I could feel a physical substance entering my aura. This was unexpected and I opened my eyes wide in surprise. Afterwards I couldn't help making a comment, one I won't repeat here.

On my way home I felt my grandfather's presence very strongly, and I wondered what had made him want to be a part of my team. The therapist had said that he knew what was coming and that he wanted to contribute. What was in front of me? I was constantly on a journey of discovery, and I had more than enough with what was going on in the present, what was around the next corner was not in my mind. I had become more concerned with learning about what shaped the moment, than with what lay ahead in the future. Now I wondered.

Before I started writing this book, I asked for my grandfather's permission to reveal the family's secret. The answer I received was that nothing is hidden, that was just an illusion for as long as we operated on this frequency. The dream with Mother Mary watching the earth confirmed this truth for me, along with the thoughts that I could hear from my mother during the ceremonies in the jungle. It became increasingly clear to me how we deceive ourselves all the time. The world was just a playground where we experience feelings, discover what brings us joy and happiness, and use our free will to choose wisely. We have only forgotten who we are and how we create what we want. We create pain and discomfort when we focus on the image of who we think we *need* to be. By losing touch with who we are, we end up with the perception that we must be someone who others want us to be, where our thoughts lead us into a rollercoaster. We allow the world to control how we behave instead of acting from our authentic center. We give all our power to the world, forgetting that we are the ones who are creating it.

Since I am constantly looking to understand how we create life, I have listened to a lot of interesting interviews. I wanted to have different points of view before I took a position on what felt right to me, I needed to listen to others to broaden my own perspectives. It felt as if the universe was sending me exactly those people that I needed to listen to, so that I could see my limitations. One of those who fascinated me with the way he passed on his knowledge was Mooji. He had popped up many times, but it had only been short video snippets. Now I found out that he had whole 'satsangs', on youtube. A satsang is a gathering of people where they meet with a guru, or teacher. Here they can ask questions about spiritual topics, and the guru or teacher will answer them. I began to listen to them, and I was impressed with the way he responded to the questions he was asked. It made sense when he said we needed to focus on the one observing, instead of being preoccupied with what we were watching. By asking questions about *who* is observing, we would change our focus, and eventually understand more about the observer. For a week I listened to a satsang every day, and on some days, I managed two, I just loved how he responded to the questions.

On the seventh day I was sitting relaxed listening to a satsang. Suddenly I got a flash of insight, and in that second, I watched the whole play of life. I broke out into spontaneous laughter; it was the funniest and most ridiculous thing I had ever seen. I sat up in my chair to focus back on the flash of insight, and I could see how people were running around from here to there, while I heard their thoughts spinning in their heads. They were totally confused. How on earth could we believe in those kinds of thoughts? The laughter increased as the film rolled on: that is ridiculous, I thought. No words could describe how delightfully hilarious it was to see it all from this angle. How was it possible to believe the thoughts that were telling us how worthless we are, how hopeless everything is, and how scary the world is. For many days I just laughed to myself knowing that we were none of the thoughts popping up in our minds. This was visible in the vision, and I also saw how they controlled our lives; the thoughts that we believed in created all our experiences. The laughter bubbled constantly, it was enough to simply remember the movie in my mind and a new wave of laughter came bursting out. It was good that no one was around, they would probably have locked me up somewhere in a second.

After this revelation I felt great ease and joy. I had heard several enlightened people talk about the joy coming forth after they discovered the truth, and I wondered many times when it might happen to me. Now I went around smiling considering nothing as a problem, just as I did in 1991. It was enough for me to recall the image of people running around in complete confusion, and completely devoid of the memory of who they are, then this made any difficulties that I had evaporate like dew in the morning sun. How ridiculous it was to worry. I thought of all the years behind me when the darkness had been lying tightly around covering my field, and I had been convinced of the truthfulness of the thoughts. Now it was easy to see how my childhood had shaped the perception of the world I lived in and had activated the fear of being me. I couldn't say what I wanted to say as the fear of being punished was immense, I wasn't allowed to be different than them or to say anything that my parents didn't believe.

The courage to be me grew stronger. When I found myself in situations where I had previously remained silent, I started saying what I was thinking. I was afraid to disclose my inner thoughts and many times I felt fearful of hurting someone else or of them becoming upset or angry. As I continued with more confidence, not only was it going well, but I saw that those around me started to listen. My courage to be myself increased and I became more visible. My mother had been invisible to me, and I realised that by acting the same way, I wasn't allowing others to get to know me. I felt that it was important for my children that I didn't repeat our family story, when my time came to leave this world, they were not going to wonder who I was. Although the game of life had been revealed to me, I knew that there was more. What this could be I had no idea, but there was something, I just knew it in my gut. After the revelations I had had so far, I couldn't stop here. I could probably have said that I was pleased with life as it was, and I would have lived a good life during the rest of my time here, but I wanted to get to the bottom of all my questions, so no stones could be left unturned.

Stones of Nacreous

The magic weave of life continued in joy and wonder, it was as if even the colours spoke to me, and I could never get enough of the scents of the flowers and the diversity of nature. The world had shut down while I was in a constant state of expansion, feeling like the silence was spreading outwards. Everyone stayed home as much as possible during lockdown, so the traffic calmed down, contributing to the silence. On my daily walks I met very few people, it was as if the world had gone to sleep. Every day I walked listening to the beautiful chirping of the birds while the warmth of the sun increased and made the tiny brown buds transform into green leaves. A stump which was at the edge of the woods close to the sea, became my daily meditation space. Here I could sit for a long time with the sound of water drifting against the rocks and feel the breeze against my face, the warmth was like a gift after a long winter. The notebook was always with me, and words of wisdom often came sailing in when I relaxed into the sounds around me.

This moment is the only thing that is. When I am here, fear or worry don't exist, and I feel like myself as I am. This moment has never started, nor will it ever end. It is eternal. In this eternal now, there is all that is, that which is not broken, nor dead. Time ceases, because everything is right now. When the past and future do not exist, there are no worries. The future depends on the past. When stories no longer have a hold on you, the trigger point doesn't activate, and the future has nothing to grow from. Everything is now, and it goes into eternity.

The words came by themselves, from the waves splashing against the rocks, through the breeze that made the leaves of the trees rattle, as if they were in joy, eager to sprout forth. How easy and simple life could be. Here I was able to rest, lower my shoulders and just be.

Everything entered a new phase after we were forced back to our homes. For me the lockdown made no difference, this was how life had been since I had moved away from my last husband. As I sat like this, enjoying the sight of the round rocks, worn, and polished by the wind and sea, I felt eternity. The river of time flowed through everything that was around me, like the one I saw in the vision so long ago. It was like an oasis, a piece of the world I was invited into. Without the eye, none of this would be visible. I thought about all the years when I had been battling with life, when all of this couldn't be seen from the darkness which my world had been created. Now I was just grateful for all my experiences, they were the ones who had brought out the joy and reverence of how my life is now. I would not have sat here on the stump, conscious of the deep peace, if it had not been for the struggle behind me. Life had been the most interesting one I could have experienced, like an adventurous journey where the goal was to find out who I am. I wouldn't have changed a moment even if someone had offered me the chance.

A memory appeared when I was lying in bed about to wake up. Before my daily consciousness was present, I registered that I was answering someone: "it is okay, my contract is about to end, I can do what is left." I stayed for a bit to see if I could get hold of the question in front of my response, knowing that it was about me being able to remove some of the obstacles of which I had agreed upon facing before coming to earth. It wasn't about my life being done, just about a part I had said I would be able to do. I thought of my journey so far as being made up of two parts: The first part being up to the experience in 1991, and the next one being up to this date. Now I wondered if there was a third part approaching. Perhaps the message I had had, that this was for later in life, was about what would come when the soul contract was finished?

I spoke to a person who confirmed the dream three years later, without my specifically asking. He could see that I had started a new period of growth, one that would reach further up. The first part was about the world, and to teach me to become grounded. Now I had started a time when the contact with my guides and angels would become closer, but there was something I had to finish before I could move on. When the person told me this, I remembered the dream and gave a big smile, no doubt my life had been about being present in the world. All my life I had avoided taking up residence in my body, until the shamans of the jungle began their purge of all the wilderness that had grown large and powerful around me. It was like the prince who walked through thorns to get to Sleeping Beauty. Now that job was done.

Throughout autumn I felt the familiar cramps in my back recur. That surprised me because I knew those pains had been healed, what had made them show up again? I worked a lot at the time, but that couldn't be the reason, I was sure. The pain came and went for a while without me getting a handle on where it had come from. As it escalated, I sent a message to a shaman I had had some contact with. The answer came back promptly; it was kidney stones. That hadn't been in my mind, but now I understood that it couldn't have been caused by anything else. He recommended a homeopathic medicine, and it helped relieve the pain within a few days. I began to wonder why my body was producing stones, and I sent an email to the shamans whom I had been with before in the jungle. I got to talk to them on zoom and was told that they would hold a ceremony a couple of weeks after, when they would look at the issue. Due to the time difference, it would be held whilst I was sleeping.

The day after they held the ceremony, the reason why my body produced stones popped up in my mind. The answer came like lightning from a clear sky; they came from the time when I discovered the abuse. I knew it to be true and felt the grief taking over. I knew it needed to come out of my shadow, out from the subconscious, and the time to continue the opening of Pandora's box had come once again. I also knew time had come to share my journey with the world. The thought of my grandfather came to mind, and I felt his presence come in. Was that why he had wanted to join my team? The knowledge that this is what I was here to do became strong, not to pass on the suffering, but to spread the faith that everything is possible to heal. I sighed and felt that I would rather put this away, it had healed, but I also felt that this had to be done before I could finish the story. I understood that this was what he had meant, the man who had said that there was something I had to finish.

Before I started, I had to ask permission from my grandfather to tell the story, I didn't want to awaken old wounds for the people involved. At the same time, I knew that all pains encapsulated in our nervous system had to be released, I also knew from my own experience that it was even more painful to carry them. I felt fear lingering in my stomach. Since I had always been a private person, one who didn't share much, even with those close to me, it felt extra challenging to be so open and honest. *But* I felt that this was what I was here to do, so there was no turning back. A vision which came in a dream several months earlier, appeared in my memory. Now I could understand more of what it wanted to show me.

I wander around in an area; the nature around looks as though I am in the highlands. The view is mesmerising and I can see large formations of mountains in the distance. The valley is far below, and I get the feeling of walking on a hillside with a slight slope on both sides. The terrain is devoid of vegetation with short, slightly brownish grass. It is reminiscent of Scotland's east coast, only this is located on top of a mountain. I am walking towards a small pond where I can see many stones adorning the bottom and sides. The water is clear as crystal, and in the middle of this pond a white pillar is placed, with a bust on top. It resembles an old artwork from the Roman empire. I have a piece of jewellery in my hand. The necklace is made of small, beautiful beads, and it has a large, green crystal hanging down like an amulet. I step into the water and put the chain around the neck of the Roman statue, then I walk away and turn to have another look. The necklace hangs exactly where it is supposed to and I know that when the time is ripe, the necklace will tear, and the big crystal will end up in the pond.

I turn around and move on. There are many such ponds placed around the area, and all are covered with the same stones at the bottom. None of them has pillars, except the one, and there is no one else to be seen. I feel the presence of my guide, the one I never get to see, but who is always with me. All is peaceful as I look out over the area. I turn to have a look at the pillar again; the necklace has cracked, and the stone is no longer visible. I gape in surprise and say to myself; "the time has come, the time is now." I walk towards it and into the water. It reaches up to the middle of my calf, and I bend down and start to lift the stones. I take them up one by one and admire each one. They have become so beautiful, they radiate in sparkling, pearlescent colours, and I am in awe of the change since I last looked at them. Carefully I put the stones back in place before I take up the next one.

As I am doing this, I can hear my guide calling me; "you have to come up and see, come right away." On the way out of the pond I see a shawl lying on the ground, part of it lying in the water. It is a flowing, almost transparent silk shawl, in white and clear blue, and I know that it belongs to my guide. I pick it up and go to the highest point. There I stop in amazement, paralysed by the sight; huge birds, so white they glisten in the sky, are flying towards me. As they come closer, I see that the tips of the wings are tinged with peach feathers. One by one they land in front of me where they transform into the most beautiful women with long hair cascading down their backs. The silk dresses they are wearing are as glistening white as the birds and move like waves around the body, as if they are alive when they raise their wings all the way up. They make an elegant pirouette in front of me before they fly on as birds again.

One after the other they come towards me, dance, spread their wings, and fly on. They are tall, perfect creatures, so beautiful that I stand glued to the ground. "Look where they are coming from, look where they are coming from," again I hear my guide's voice, and I lift my head to focus on the direction they come from. Once again, I am struck by the sight in front of me. Thousands of birds are heading towards me, and I see them coming from behind the mountains which I glimpse in the distance. They come directly from the bright light that shines across the sky. "Dear God," I pray, "please give me something I can take with me, so I know this is true." I look down at the ground where I see a pile of feathers lying in front of me, they are shiny white with peach tips. The joy flows through me as I thank God, "it is true, this is true." The feeling is not possible to put into words, I am totally filled with amazement and gratitude, and the joy is rippling through all my veins. I take a deep breath and start walking down the hill. There I see a wrought iron bed standing between some bushes. I can see myself sitting upright in bed while my mouth moves constantly. I go closer so that I can listen to what I am saying. After listening for some seconds, I shake my head and exclaim: "I don't want to listen to you anymore," turn around, and start walking in the direction of where the birds came from.

When I woke up, I stayed quiet for a long time, memorising every detail. I felt a huge peace, and there was like a holiness left in the room from the visitation. I knew that this was the most important vision I had ever had up to that point, and I knew that I needed some time to understand the depth of it. I had been sick during the last week with some virus infecting my lungs, and I hadn't been able to get out of bed until the day following the dream. It was two months prior to the world announced pandemic. In the evening I attended a gathering on zoom, where Michael Tamura was hired as a guest speaker. I had been listening to many of the stories he had shared on youtube, after his five near death experiences, and the wisdom he conveyed I found inspiring. When I talked to him, I asked if I could share a dream that I had had that morning, and when I finished my sharing, he looked at me and exclaimed; "congratulations, when you started telling me about your dream, the colour of your aura changed and turned completely purple." He went on to say that this reminded him of his third near death experience, where he had looked down on an ocean of seraphs. They are the angels who are closest to God's throne, along with the cherubim, as they say in the bible. It was incredibly good to get confirmation from someone, who himself was versed in 'the other side' and had great experience. My assumption during the meditation in the morning, was that they had come to walk me home. Then I couldn't be that far away, could I?

Archangel Michael

I hadn't been that sick for many years, but I managed to stay up from the day after my dream. Another week of recovery passed so I had plenty of time to dwell on the dream's message. When the pandemic hit, I knew that it was the message which I had received when the crystal fell into the water; the time had come, the turnaround the world needed to get back to a way of life in harmony with nature and with love, had started. The fear radiating from everyone I met was palpable, it was as if the media and people were getting a sensational kick, and the adrenaline in free flow enhanced the fears. I was completely calm, and I knew that everything was as it should be.

A dream which I had had in my late twenties also appeared in my mind and gave me a new meaning. During the years of my first marriage, I had many dreams where a guide had shown up. He came every time I wondered what to do, and what choice to make to resolve the difficulties I was in. The guy showing up in my dreams was a beautiful young man, tall and with golden hair. His radiation was androgynous, as if the feminine part was in balance with the masculine. He instilled confidence and I always felt relief when he showed up, then I knew that I was safe and would get the help I needed. Often, he came whilst I was at an intersection wondering which path to take, and the signs I was looking at went in all directions. When he showed up, I just looked at him and followed his back as he walked ahead. There was never any communication between us, just a mutual understanding,

I needed guidance, and he came to assist. It was after the last dream where he appeared that I understood his identity: he was Archangel Michael. This is the last dream where he showed up, which came into mind when the pandemic hit. It appeared in my mid-twenties, almost forty years ago.

I become aware that I am walking up a road and it ends up in front of an intersection. As I am studying the signs and wondering which path to take, I see my guide walking towards me. I am happy and relieved that he has come to show me which road to take, and I begin to follow him as he walks with steady steps up the hill. He chooses neither of the roads this time and we walk up a grassy hill. Now I can see that we are approaching a mountain wall. As we reach the foot of the mountain wall, I look up at the top towering high above us, wondering how I am going to get there. He points to an area where there are some bushes, and I walk towards it to have a look. There I see the opening of a cave, well hidden by vegetation, and I go inside it. There I see an elevator and I enter. It goes right up, and in a second, I am at the top. Once on the plateau I walk straight over to the edge where railings are set up, and I look out on the landscape below me. There are meadows and crows as far as I can see, areas where trees separate the patches of land, and far in the distance I get a glimpse of blue mountains. Farmhouses are scattered around, and the roads intersect in some places. A cluster of houses tells me that there is a village nearby. Cars rush along the roads, and I can see people walking.

Far away on the horizon I suddenly see a huge tsunami coming towards us, and I know why my guide showed me the way up here. This is a safe place to be, the tsunami cannot reach where I am standing. It looks like a hundred-meter wall of water rolling towards us and I can see the people far down start to run here and there in complete confusion and terror. There is nowhere to hide, and I can feel the fear from them wafting in the air. I know that everyone who has made it up here is safe, and the wave can't reach us. My daughter stands next to me, and I see my son running towards the mountain wall while he looks up to us. I point to the opening, and he gets in and into safety too. As the water rushes in all over the area the three of us stand and watch it from above.

It was a special dream, very vivid, and I wondered for a long time what it was trying to tell me. Since I was unable to decipher it, I put it in the archive and completely forgot about it. A year ago, it reappeared in my memory, and I understood that it showed the time that would come, the time we are in now. With the pandemic spreading like a flood around the world, fear has taken over many people's lives. We look for hiding places to avoid being infected by the virus, but there are no places to go, the virus mutates, and the vaccines are not working. Water in my dreams, I know, is about emotions, and what I felt from the people I saw was great fear. Those of us who stood above the wave were not touched by the fear spreading through the world because we knew we were safe.

One day at the beginning of the lockdown I strolled down to my favourite place by the water. I wanted to contemplate the latest visions and the dream that had reappeared. No place was better than 'my' stump, and every time I came, I noticed something new. It was as if the absence of people was giving nature new life. Everything abounded in abundance, even the snakes seemed to increase in number. Now I could smile at my former fears, the trips to the jungle had cured most of them although I had no need to seek out the small creatures. I walked calmly as I looked down occasionally so I wouldn't step on anyone. Suddenly I froze, something had stopped me, and I was standing with one heel on the ground ready to step down on the rest of my foot. I didn't know what had made me stop so immediately and looked down, there I saw a snake moving at full speed under my foot. Had nothing stopped me I would have stepped on it. I sent up a thank you note, saying that they had prevented me from harming the snake, and I strolled even more carefully afterwards.

The closeness I felt to divinity was more intimate than ever, it was as if many people were walking with me when I was outside. I felt the presence of a cloak around my body and my senses were opening like rosebuds in the warmth of sunshine. When I allowed myself to rest in the silence my inner vision was activated, it was as if I could see beyond matter, and what I saw was life. The vision of the power going through everything that is here, came alive again. The image of my person sitting in bed babbling kept popping up. I smiled and I agreed that there were a lot of strange words coming out of that mouth, now I could feel that there was another part taking over more and more: the eternal part of me. My soul showed me what was true, but my head needed time to surrender. The world view had been greatly imprinted from the time I had lain in my mother's womb. Now I had more trust in my inner guidance than I had in my thoughts, which shifted from one moment to the next.

Sounds from the Soul

When I allowed myself to trust what was coming, to believe in my inner visions and downloads, a new security emerged. Although I couldn't share the certainty with the outside world, I knew that I was waking up something inside myself which had been dormant, just like Sleeping Beauty when the prince woke her up after a hundred years. Had I told my friends and family what I was experiencing, it would have just been an extra struggle with arguments and a need to defend my point of view. The world around me couldn't see what I saw, it could just be activated in my inner chamber. This awakening required calmness and silence so the small bud could grow strong. Who am I really? Many times, I stood in front of the mirror and looked into my own eyes wondering. My good bio-resonance therapist, who had now sadly (for me) gone home, had said many times while looking directly at me; "I wonder who you are. Imagine if there was a zipper on you so we could open it and have a look." He who could see and talk to the archangels, Jesus, and other light beings, what could *he* see? Every time the comment came as he looked at me, I got a strange feeling which I couldn't identify, I left with the question ringing in my ears. "Who am I?" A vision I had a couple of years earlier often appeared when I dwelt on this.

I am inside a golden light and it is the most beautiful place I have ever seen. The music floating around me is so breathtakingly beautiful it feels as if I am in an eternal flow of bliss. My gaze sweeps around, and I see an opening further ahead. I slide forward to the edge of it, watching the light move downwards in a spiral. A line of notes flows out of a tapestry that I see like a wave floating horizontally on my left side, that is where the music comes from. There is no beginning nor end to the web of notes I see, and it flows like a river in a golden-purple light. There is an ecstasy of joy and love in everything, as if even the air vibrates in this. I know that all the notes come from souls living on earth, and the music is created through their connection with us, it is the vibration of every soul sending their prayers. As I stand on the edge of the golden spiral, I see beings of light throwing themselves downhill with great joy and delight, and they sail down in the stream of the spiral.

Then I become aware of something behind me, and I am drawn to it like a magnet. There I am left staring at a dark area in the tapestry, and I see that it comes from a time when many souls lost touch with their origins, with themselves. Their tones can no longer be heard in heaven, the voices from many souls are not able to reach through the darkness which they are experiencing. All the notes are equally important, the music is not complete until everyone is heard. I can see whilst studying the black spot that they have lost their way and have forgotten who they are. The pain chases like a scream through me, and I know it is God's pain which is rippling through my entire being. His despair for the souls who are living in an absence of contact, in total darkness and despair, has no limits. All the beauty disappears, the only thing that matters is the pain which these souls are feeling. They long for home, home to love. I cry out from the depths of my soul; "what can I do to help?"

The second that I express the thought I am shot out like a beam of light, and the next moment I find myself in front of a higher self. It is stunningly beautiful. A whole bunch of dna threads, too many for me to count, are meandering and writhing in an amazing dance. This being is so full of life with all the colours of the rainbow swirling around, whilst sparkling and flashing like fireworks. I am studying this phenomenon, and one dna thread after another extends out before going back to its place. One thread contains a life as a Native American, another shows me a life of a gypsy. I stand there for a long time; it is like I am inculcating all the lives contained by this higher self.

I became conscious of myself again, of the weight of my body resting heavily on the mattress. I was speechless. What had I been taking part in now? I couldn't tell anyone; they would think I had gone crazy. The experience of an *I* had never been stronger, and it was not possible to construct this fantasy. I have always been fond of daydreaming, especially in my childhood, but day dreams as lush and rich as the movie I just had experienced, my imagination wouldn't have been able to create. The colours had been magical, like watercolours that slipped into each other and erased all contours. It was as if the music was in the colours, and even the air was alive. I couldn't get up yet, I wanted to just lie in this magical atmosphere and memorise as much as possible. I tried to remember the lives which had been shown to me so clearly, but the only ones I could bring into my conscious awareness were those lives of a Native American and a gypsy. This made me remember a woman who used to draw people's auras. When I had had an appointment with her in my late twenties, she had drawn a Native American pattern beneath me, explaining that it was the foundation I had brought with me into this life. This life contained all the resources that I would need to have. She also told me that the life as a gypsy was one of the lives which I had brought with me to heal. Life was strange.

I knew that I had been home with God, where I had been prior to coming to earth. The pain I felt was easy to remember and it was immense. Was this the moment that I had made the decision to come here now? I thought about the world around me. I had no doubt that God was swept aside. All that people believed in was to get an education so that they could earn as much money as possible. Materialism was the only thing that we gave importance to, and that was what made us feel worthy. Where I had just been, peace and harmony, along with an ineffable bliss, were the only absolute truths. Was it possible to bring this truth into the world? If little me could contribute I would do anything, I would happily be ridiculed if only one person found himself, I could do anything that contributed to the heavenly music being complete. The pain of the souls who had forgotten their sound was too real for me to ignore.

While I was lying contemplating what I had seen, another dream came sailing into my memory. It had been many years since it had appeared, and I wondered if it had any connection to this last vision.

I am on my way up a small stone staircase, towards a big, old, wooden door, it is a door at the back of an old, brick, mansion. We are five people sightseeing in England, visiting places known to hold strong energies. We go inside and enter a huge hall. A pharyngeal passage goes around the entire room, and I can see many doors along the walls up on the first floor. A big opening in the floor in front of me arouses my curiosity and I go closer to explore what it is. A deep shaft comes into view, and it feels bottomless. I know that I have found the 'Devil's den', and amazingly I manage to keep standing to look down into it. Windows are lined up, all with curtains and flowerpots. They go in a spiral and follow the shaft downwards. Behind every window I know that families are living their lives, and that they are unaware of their captivity. I feel a deep sense of despair that the devil has deceived them. The light shines down some distance, but then the darkness gets denser and denser until it becomes total blackness. Where there is still light people can be saved, but I know that those who have come too far down are lost. I need help to close the den so that the devil can't escape into the world, and I rush off to get more help, I know that this work requires many helping hands. I come back with many people, and we start to build a glass pyramid on top of the hole. When it is finished, I breathe a sigh of relief, I know that we are safe. I can see that the tip of the pyramid towers all the way up to the ceiling and that the tip of it is placed exactly above the den.

Was the shaft the same as the dark spot I had seen in the tapestry floating in space? I wondered. What did all these visions and dreams want to tell me? Each one was so vivid and colourful, it was as if I was sitting in a movie theatre, in the middle of a 3D movie, and they showed up like trolls out of a box, without warning. The trips to the jungle, conversations with people I had met, dreams, visions, and OBEs, (out-of-body experiences), all of these had changed everything that I had previously thought. When I put all this together, I could see that there was a thread which was linking them all together, but I needed to understand more with my mind. Where would this lead? All the downloads with insights, all the above mentioned, really made me question what was true and what wasn't.

As I have mentioned before, it took me a couple of years before I could start to accept what I had seen to be true, but the vision of the place with the beautiful music sometimes came in when I was contemplating who I am. Little by little it opened like the petals of a flower on its way to bloom, it was as if I had to take one step at a time, and when I was familiar with what I understood the next thing could be shown to me. After the sight of the higher self, consisting of living dna threads, I had no doubt that all the lives affected each other all the time. As inside so outside, as above so below, as in heaven so on earth. All these metaphors we were throwing around now became alive, I understood what they meant. Our bodies are designed through programmes in our dna, and life is designed in the dna of the higher self. This dna is not static. It is dynamic and constantly changing and expanding. When I changed a conviction that I had held as true, everything else changed. When my new ideas were in accordance with God's laws, I made room for more of what is my real self to open and expand my view. The limiting beliefs instilled in me whilst I was growing up made me close down; my opinions could not be received and were called fantasy. The punishment for saying something wrong, or something which was not accepted by my dad, silenced me, and eventually made me doubt myself. This had followed me all my life, creating the cave in which I existed. Was this the devil's cave? Even with everything that was shown to me, I hesitated to open, it was scary. The world's perception, like the queen in the fairytale of Snow White consulting the mirror, had a strong grip.

Imagine what life would be like if everyone was allowed to say what they see and hear, without being punished for it or ridiculed. The suffering comes when we close off our hearts, when we have lost touch with ourselves. When I studied the dark spot, I looked straight into hell. This is a state where we have lost contact with ourselves, and this is where I chose to go to overcome it. Doing the work has enabled me to recognise when others have closed themselves off. When people come to me for help visions open and I can see where the blockages are stored. By removing my own blinkers and anything which has been limiting my way of perceiving the world, I have opened the channels. There I have access to talk to the team who have been helping me, and together we are strong. I also know this doesn't just apply to me; we are all here to do this work. Everyone can return to the little voice inside, but they must choose to go on that path. We are all sisters and brothers, created by our father/mother whom I call God. The beautiful stones I had admired in the pond where the pillar was located, each one kept its own story. The pearlescent, glittering colours, came from transformed pain. They were stories that had framed my existence, and from which I had released the pain and hurt. Doing this work I changed each stone (story) into big pearls.

Justice

As previously mentioned, the principle of justice has always been primary for me. All the injustice I had felt as a child had made me aware of how I didn't want to behave as an adult. An episode came out loud and clear as I was writing about the subject some time ago. I was eight years old when it happened. The whole street was filled with friends of all ages, and we were an active bunch who always had a lot of fun. My brother's friend was going to celebrate his birthday and he had invited everyone except me, even my best friend was going to the party. I was inconsolable and asked my mother why I was not invited. What had I done? My brother and his comrade were only one year older than me, so I didn't understand why this happened. My mother couldn't give me an explanation, but she said that she was going to sew a nice coat for my barbie doll while the others were at the party. I remember sitting next to her as she sewed a green modern coat with white fur edgings. Although I was grateful for what she did, I understood that she felt sorry for me, the pain was intense. It was an injustice I couldn't swallow.

Since I was a girl, I had never been allowed to do many of the things my brother was allowed to do, which felt deeply unfair too. The last slap I had been given by my father came after my brother was allowed to visit friends one Saturday afternoon, whilst I was forbidden to go out. I asked why and got the answer that I was a girl and had to be at home more than he was. Then I cursed, which was *not* allowed, and my father instantly gave me a slap which sent my glasses to the other side of the room. During my life I have experienced many unfair incidents, whilst at the same time focusing on treating others fairly. Now this picture also began to change. I could see how my focus created the exact opposite of what I wanted. As I understood more about the laws of creation, I could see that my sense of justice came from a dualistic view, it was divided. When I felt the pain of not being asked to the party, I became angry at the one who didn't ask me. The injustice came from an egocentric notion of wanting to be treated the same way as my friends. Of course, this is not wrong, it is important to create equality in a group of friends, but I could now see the whole episode from another perspective.

When looking at the term, justice, from my new understanding, I could see that what I considered to be fair, in truth had included a judgment. When my father said that I could not be treated as equal to my brother, it was my anger that was activated. It is not ok to treat someone in this way, but I could see that what I had created for myself was worse. My judgment of others was obscured by the concept of injustice, so I had to really reverse my perception when it came into my sight so clearly. If I acted from my dualistic point of view, then I would create the opposite of what I wanted. The world is not fair, and it never will be for as long as we look from this perspective, at the same time there is a justice that will always rule, which is as we sow, so shall we reap.

What is perceived as okay for one person may be the opposite for another, but the laws of life cannot be passed by. They are constant, and we do not have an overview of what applies to others. We can only sweep our own doorstep. When I send out a thought that is not in accordance with the universal laws, or I act contrary to them, I must pay the consequences. I had had the experience of existing in total love. Even all the things my first husband did to me in anger or jealousy, were perfectly fine inside that love. His actions were not my business. My job was not to react against those actions in anger and frustration. "When you are hit on your left cheek, give forth your right cheek." Now I understood what Jesus meant. He spoke from truth and the laws of the universe, and knew what he was teaching. He saw what the actions they took created for themselves and refused to take part in those creations. The love that I was in encompassed everything, there was no difference between friend and foe.

It is important to clarify that there should be a law and order we can relate to. If we live in a society where there is a focus on material goods and powers, we cannot let everything sail along unhindered. Once the world's communities experience the same love that was in me, we wouldn't need a courtroom. Then we will be able to live with the best intentions for ourselves and our neighbours. This will change all our thoughts and actions. From this mindset I would have been invited to the birthday party, my father wouldn't have treated me the way he did, and we would all act from a place of wanting everyone to be as happy as oneself.

It will take a few generations until we get there, but I am positive about the way forward. More and more people are changing their values in how they live their lives. Through the chaos we experience now, the old structures are collapsing. Since the pandemic started a lot has changed. Many people relocated from big cities and are choosing to work from home as much as possible. This frees up time with children and family, and we have become more aware of how much being together really means. We use the phrase, there is no justice in the world, and no, there is not, and it never will be from our current perspective. Real justice will become alive when we live from the heart. We must exchange the laws of the world for the laws of creation. We must become aware of which of these laws we operate within, God's justice will always apply.

The Pain of the World

As the days of spring leaned more and more toward summer, and I could feel how the warmth from the breeze increased each day, it made me sigh pleasantly as I strolled slowly along the trail. The trees had become deep green, and the beautiful, light green colour they had in the beginning was now just a memory. What a gift it was to be able to follow nature's awakening. Every day brought something new to admire, bluebells took over after the windflowers were done, the summer flowers appeared, contributing to a richer colour range the more the heat took hold. I took a deep breath and enjoyed the scent of pine and soil, and looking around the fields I could see a wealth of summer flowers sprouting out in all their splendid forms. Each time I saw this view, I was reminded of my childhood summers in the north where gardens and roadsides were full of the most beautiful summer flowers, which I loved to pick. After picking a bouquet I would run at full speed back home so that my mother could put them in a glass of water. I had to smile at the thought, and I couldn't remember ever experiencing bad weather.

It was lovely to feel the warmth of the sun as I walked, my mind was in a state of rest, and everything was peaceful. My gaze wandered across the field towards a cluster on the other side and suddenly it was like the mirror disappeared: I recognised the moment. I was supposed to be right here, right now. The picture I saw had existed before I came here, I remembered, I had caught up with this moment. I stopped in amazement, no thoughts existed, just a state of being. The last few months I had had so many of them, I now just stopped and was present with the experience. The moment was like the white stones Hansel and Gretel picked, and then dropped on the road on their way into the woods. These signs would help them find their way back home and to know they were on the right track. These moments gave me the same confirmation, I was exactly where I was supposed to be, I was on the right path. As I strolled home, I pondered the concept of déjà vu. What was it really? I knew it was a recognition of the moment, like a reverberation from the universe, but why did it appear?

Once I got home, I made myself a cup of coffee, and wanted to have a short scroll on Facebook before I started the day's doings. The first thing that showed up was a citation from Michael Tamura where he wrote about déjà vu. I had to laugh to myself, the universe didn't take long to answer me. He wrote that it is we who can already see, and that all déjà vu is clairvoyance, that is, I recognise the moment because I have already seen it. Then my first understanding was not too far out. When my mind didn't take over, reality could come into view, and then I would remember. I was laughing at myself, not only because of what I read, but just as much because the answer I sought came in front of me so quickly. What a magical world, synchronicities came like pearls on a string.

Everything I had experienced caused my whole worldview to crumble. The fear the media was spreading around felt like a physical stabbing against my skin when I was out in public. For me it was just events on the stage of life, even though I followed most of the restrictions and commandments. I didn't want to add more fear to people around me, but for me the world was more like a 'fata morgana', a mirage, its solidity, and impenetrability were gone. What was real was on the inside and not what I saw out there. Collectively we had created everything that was going on, but I was sure that when it was over, the world would be a better place than before. How long this would take would be left unsaid, but I knew we needed this reorganisation, I had no doubt. During all the chaos going on around the world, I had two dreams the same night. The first one waking me up after just two hours sleep, like something was demanding me to write it down.

I am waiting for the sign to board a ferry. My car is at the front of the last line that will be ushered in and there is no one behind me. Right in front of the car I see my oldest grandson with a friend. Both have bikes and both have one foot on the ground and the other ready on the pedal. I am looking at the cars driving in and I am watching as the rows fill up one plateau before they get hoisted up and the next group is brought in. Several floors are now in place and the only one left is the ground floor. It is very narrow with little space up to the roof and I am relieved that I have a sports car, or else I wouldn't fit.

The ferryman waves me forward gesturing to the right side of the boat. I am surprised because this leads me away from the driveway into the ferry and out onto the quay. I know I am supposed to go into the boat. Since I always follow the messages given to me, I follow where he points. I give a sign to the boys that they must move, and they get ready to ride. I slowly sneak forward following the boys, and as it takes some time for them to move, I haven't rolled many meters before the ferryman gives a sign to go inside. I breathe a sigh of relief and turn my car the right way. As I drive further into the boat, I can feel the weight of all the cars parked above me very strongly. They feel like a huge heaviness on my shoulders as I move further and further in.

The tunnel I am driving inside is slightly curving to the left, so I am not able to see the end of it. After a while I start to wonder when I will be at the end whilst at the same time the feeling of the weight over me is getting lighter. I understand that I am past all the cars and approaching where I am supposed to park. A clear blue sky appears, and I stop in front of a large gate. I get out of the car to wait at the side of it while crossing the river, I know it won't be long until we are over. I see a glimpse of green grass as a vision which indicates we are getting close. Flowers of all colours and a bright light comes into sight when we get close to the other side. I know the gate will open as soon as we reach the shore and that I will be the first to drive into the land, all the other cars will automatically follow. I wake up with a dash of 'yes, I made it,' and with full knowledge that all is well.

The next morning, I woke up early with another dream alive in front of me.

I am about to arrive at a retreat with a lot of people. The venue is in a beautiful garden and the flowers are in full bloom, a lovely aroma surrounds me as I open the door of the car and I walk towards the building, I meet a small group of five people who will assist me in the work. We walk into the building, and I see a chair placed on a stage. I go and sit down and watch while people come in and find their seats, they have come to listen to the channelling that is taking place. When all is ready, I close my eyes and focus on my breathing. The surroundings slip away and after a short time I hear light snoring sounds, and I know this is a sign that I am out of my body and ready to start. I feel a huge heaviness enter and take over my body. The moment that it does I start talking, and a huge sorrow and deep pain emerges. Those sitting around me start taking notes as I talk. My tears start to flow, I cry over the pain that people are feeling in their lives, the despair I feel they carry. I tell them this is not what we are here to experience. We are here to have fun, to experience the physical life with play and laughter. I talk and cry, the heavy pain of people's suffering that flows through me feels like a straitjacket weighing me down. During the break it is a relief to be back to myself and let go of the suffering. I look at the people who are chatting and enjoying themselves in the garden. After the break I guide them through an exercise where they drop the loads that they have been carrying. Then I awake.

I stayed for a while in bed contemplating both dreams, pondering what connection they had with each other. The cars parked on floors above me on the ferry felt like lead weights over my head. The only living people I could see were the boys who continued their journey into life and the ferryman. The others were safely placed in their cars during the crossing. I was alive and with a knowledge that they would be free when we were on the other side, and that the work I was doing would eventually bear fruit. Why did the ferryman wave me away from the driveway at first? Was there anything I needed to change my focus on? It was almost as if I hadn't made it, and I knew I *had* to enter the ferry. The dreams were so strong and vivid, that even now when I write about them more than one year after, I can feel the feelings that were activated.

The last dream was not difficult to understand. The pain I had felt in this dream was the same as in the vision where I had felt God's pain, studying the living tapestry, it was heavy. The despair over the notes that couldn't be heard is one of the most intense feelings that I have had, and it is as present now as it was then. It confirmed my recent thoughts, that this is why I am here. The weight of what had entered me was palpable, it felt as if an energy ball had taken over my being. The dream also helped me to acknowledge the vision that I had had in the past, where the notes that emanated from the tapestry were what gave life to the colours floating in the air. Each time a memory appeared new layers of insight revealed themselves. Well, if some of it was true all of it had to be true, even the part where I was shot out of the sky and appeared in front of my higher self where I was inculcating the lives that it contained.

Since I could see myself, I could not be the person who had lived the lives I had been watching, no one can see themselves they can only be, we need mirrors to see ourselves. I chose to go into the lives that this higher self had contained to help the world. Ah, I thought, then the answer I got from a guide I had had that time, was true. After I got home from the jungle, I asked him why I was shown pictures of myself up to two years of age, and not all the years. From that age and upwards, all came as a clarity regarding what the medicine was working on, and not as movies. I also had a strange experience a few months after coming home while I was on an airplane. I covered my face with my hands whilst sighing; is this really possible? I got a flashback where I saw myself lying curled up in a cave, another dream a lifetime ago. It seemed that in this life I had to break free of every single belief I had ever had. My consciousness had to expand a lot in one single lifetime. The moment in which I had given myself the promise to find out the truth, I hadn't known what I had been journeying into. I couldn't help but accept the experiences that I had been given and continue the ride. Where would this end?

The Living Library

As I have mentioned before, I wondered many times why the pictures had been so clear until I was two years old. It had been like watching a movie rolling in front of me, and at the same time I was the little girl too. I could feel all her feelings, the influence of the environment, and the effects it activated in me. Some months after I had reached home, I decided to see if I could find answers as to why I was allowed to see only up to two years of age. I sat down to meditate and asked the question to Erik Medhus, who was present at the time, and went into a deep silence. Erik Medhus is a young guy who shot himself, and that started to help many human beings after his mother let him talk through mediums.

It didn't take long before I could feel the presence coming in and I listened. *"Until you were two years you were not totally in the body and the memories that you were supposed to heal were in your cells. For you to process and forgive, to release the energies your cells were holding onto, you needed to know where they came from. After this time, it was possible for you to remember without watching the images. You processed what had needed to be transformed with the knowledge of what it was all about, without needing to see. If we had allowed later images to come in, you would have needed healing for them too."* The voice quietened down, and again I became aware of myself.

I was left sitting without a thought for a long time. I had not expected this. I had barely heard about the walk-in concept, was I a walk-in? Over the next few days, I read what I could find about the term. Wikipedia's explanation was that there is a change of souls, one soul leaves the body, and another takes over. I thought that this sounded strange so I needed some time to digest it and see what would turn up. I know when something is true for me, and I know that the guide didn't want to mislead me at any point, my head had trouble in accepting it though. What happened in my first two years will be revealed in my next book, as I just learned what was going on.

A few months later I went to a retreat in Amsterdam. It had the title 'Awaken your Illuminated Heart', designed by Drunvalo Melchizedek. He is a Canadian that has written many books such as 'the flower of life', and he has been investigating into what consciousness is and ancient historie. The course was a powerful experience. The meditations and tasks left deep traces, as if I got even further into the layers I am carrying. On the plane on my way home something unexpected happened. It was packed, but luckily, I had my seat facing the aisle. The other two seats were occupied by big men who needed space, so I made myself as small as I could and put on the earphones. The energy was tight, so I wanted to listen to some calm meditation music and to disconnect from my surroundings.

On the way up into the air I heard a buzzing sound, it sounded like a huge bumblebee whizzing right over me. It came closer as if coming from afar, and I felt my body begin to vibrate. Something was coming towards me, but I didn't know what it could be. I closed my eyes and focused on the vibration. A strong despair appeared, and I wanted to cry. I hoped that the man sitting beside me hadn't noticed my struggle and I tried to sit as still as possible. Fortunately, I was able to hold back the tears by breathing calmly and gently, then a movie started rolling in my mind.

I am in the southern house where I used to go in my sleep as a child. I am an adult at this time, and for the first time I can see myself standing up on the porch. Behind me, inside the house, I know that there are many souls waiting for their turn to travel. Now I am waiting to be picked up, and it feels like I must leave earlier than I had planned. I dreaded going because I knew it wouldn't be an easy road. I look out over a beautiful landscape, and on the horizon, I can see a dark cloud coming towards me. It comes closer and it increases in scope, at the same time the vibration of the sound hightens in its intensity. Suddenly I am swallowed up by the darkness and I am gone. Everything becomes quiet, the sound and vibration stop instantly when the darkness takes over.

I sank heavily back into the chair, overwhelmed by what I had seen, the knowledge of what was unfolding came together with the vision. Erik Medhus, who told me that I was a walk-in, was telling the truth. I just had to accept it. (To be followed up in my next book). This affected all my preconceived notions about who we are as human beings. The darkness I saw coming towards me must have contained the soul that had entered this body at birth. It must be a soul agreement before entering the physical life, if we are to come in as walk-ins. Maybe the energy was so low that I had to step in earlier? I was speechless for the rest of the trip, while the experience stayed with me.

The tapestry that I saw in my vision with the dark spot, was without a beginning or an end. It really contained much more than my brain could perceive or believe. After the vision I realised that it was the living library called the Akashic records, where all information is stored. Was it from the living library that all dreams and visions came? Was what I saw coded and gradually released so that my head would be able to take it in? I couldn't tell anyone about this, I thought again, and I wished that I had had someone to guide me through all the experiences. My search for truth caused my mind to be chaotic and confused at times, and the beliefs that I had carried throughout my life were very fragmented. I was still me, but the understanding of me was constantly changing. As soon as I came to terms with a new concept something else appeared, and I had to rearrange my thoughts and beliefs again. Would I ever reach the goal? Did a goal even exist? It seemed that everything was in a perpetual expansion and unfolding without an end.

Life was as it had always been outwardly speaking. I went shopping, cooked, visited family and friends, worked, all the things we all do here. At the same time, it was as if I was seeing it from a totally different perspective than others. I no longer felt like a human being, rather a soul inhabiting a human body. I understood Jesus' words; "be in the world, but not of it." The life that I lived was my own creation, and when something unforeseen happened I knew that it was a gift to understand something I hadn't previously understood. I knew everything was happening *for* me and never *against* me. Where I used to feel frustration or resentment, those feelings had completely gone. It felt like the layers of the goose where everything bounces off. It didn't mean my feelings were off, rather that they were good, and the love I had for everything and everyone, increased. All that previously had been unpleasant or difficult was now inside the sphere of love.

The spider's web couldn't catch me because I was no longer in a battle with life. I realised that the more I accepted in me, the more I was able to accept in others. I know that we are all on a journey to find out who we are, and no one can know what is best for someone else. I can see how we interact in the creation of life and every time we meet a resistance we are meeting with a limitation. We have the choice of how we react. Now that this was so clear to me, what had clouded my seeing? I know there are beliefs that stem from both heritage and environment. The experience which I had thirty years ago was the beginning of looking at life from a wider perspective. That was when

I awoke to possibilities I hadn't seen before, but that I realised were there, and all my experiences outside the physical felt more real than my usual physical life. I know that without these experiences my life would have been a deplorable chapter. A dream which I had had in the middle of my twenties helped me to walk the steps I needed to move forward. My life at that time had been in great despair and pain, physically and mentally, and I had wondered many times how I was going to cope. Every day I thought about what to do and how I could improve my life. One night a dream came through, and I preserved it as a treasure within.

I am inside an old barn and the walls are grey with age. The double doors are both open and I look out at the green grass. It sparkles in the sun, and I can see summer flowers abounding in many colours out there. Inside where I am sweeping the floor, it is dark and dim. The sunlight outside can't get through the dust swirling up each time I use the broom. I must clean everything before I can go out into the beautiful summer day. As I am doing the job, I suddenly see a man walking towards me. He is tall and beautiful, and his hair is dark like ebony. He comes up to me and reaches out his hand. As he opens it, I see a wedding ring glittering towards me. I have a look at it, and I know that he wants me to accept it. I shake my head with the answer: "I can't accept it yet; I have to finish my work." He disappears and I continue to sweep the floor.

The work never ends, what I do makes no difference. After a few moments the man returns and extends his hand once again, the wedding ring glows towards me. I look at his hand and I want so much to take the ring, but I shake my head once again, the work is not done so I cannot accept it. Again, I am alone. The dust swallows all light, and I must finish. The air is just as thick as it was before I started, and now I begin to feel totally exhausted, will I never be done? I want to give up and I feel that my strength is running out. All the work I am doing, and it still doesn't make any difference no matter how hard I work. Before long the man returns for the third time.

When he reaches out and shows me the ring again, I can feel that I won't be able to finish the work in the barn, I am too tired. I extend my hand and take it, and as soon as I hold it in my hand, the summer comes pouring in, filling the entire room. The green grass takes over and the dust and darkness disappear. The flowers and scents from them vibrate in my nose and an intense joy makes my smile grow. The sun is beaming, and the dark room is gone as if it had never existed. The roof of the barn disappears and is replaced by a clear blue sky. The fatigue is blown away like it has never been present.

I woke up with an indescribably beautiful feeling, it was as if all despair had been exchanged for ecstatic joy. It took some minutes before I came completely back into myself and the world that I lived in. I remember thinking this was what the future was holding, showing me everything was going to be fine. A new hope was engendered, and I had confidence in what was to come. Even though life was still difficult I felt something deep inside me shift. I sensed a new strength coming forth, one that hadn't been there when I had gone to bed the night before; it gave me courage to keep going.

Effervescent Champagne Bubbles

The puzzle pieces of life began to fall more and more into place, and it felt like there couldn't be many pieces left. When old dreams popped into my memory, I knew that they had come to show me something I hadn't understood before. The little turn where I almost didn't get on to the ferry had stayed in my head. What was it that had almost made me miss the ferry in my dream? I saw life as creative movements where beautiful patterns were always changing, like a mosaic painting in perpetual expansion, like the stargazer I loved as a kid. When I stared into it and turned the wheel amazing images changed their colours and patterns. I could sit for hours enjoying the sights of eternal play. Now it was time to find the last piece, the one that would make the picture complete. The pursuit of positive feelings was now coming from the inside, and the joy I was used to feeling every time I had bought something nice meant nothing. I understood how fleeting this was.

My search for happiness was directed inwards and not in the constant fluctuation of the outside world. After love had washed through me in 1991, I changed the lens from which I looked at the world. I had a completely new perspective that had emerged from this experience, and all my problems started to disappear as if they had never existed. Being with my children, good relationships, and loving gatherings, became more important than doing something that didn't connect with my heart. What I owned or not, was not on the plate. My budget was tight, but I managed and then it was okay. I didn't worry, which had been my constant experience in the past, joy bubbled in my chest, and nothing seemed like a problem.

Now I could see how life's difficulties removed me from this inner experience of peace and joy. When the focus was outwards, I could feel the magnetic pull drawing me back into old patterns and disturbing my harmony. These insights required constant attention to balance my inner and outer world. When the secrets opened about my abuse, my inner knowledge became the anchor that I clung to. Without that I wouldn't have made it. I needed the knowledge of the unseen, and felt the energies around me giving me balm and support for when the storm outside me took place. The questions I asked activated the seeker, and the search for answers could begin. The dreams came back to uncover new layers and they helped me to see how guided I was. It was as if my inner search had activated my subconscious to show me more of what was stored, to make it come forward with what was hidden in the dark. This was like riddles I had to solve, just as Jesus spoke in metaphors and riddles for the uninitiated, but for the initiated his words were clear as day. Likewise, an incomprehensible dream which had changed to become as clear as daylight when I understood what it wanted to show me. What I perceived had come from the consciousness I had possessed at that moment; now new discoveries could emerge when I set aside previous convictions and old norms. Comfort zones were constantly being expanded.

In this sphere I was singing hymns from the Santo Daime songbook one evening, along with a live broadcast on youtube. I love these lyrics and melodies, and I would rather put on a recording from the church than watch television. I was completely immersed in the lyrics, floating with the atmosphere of pure rhythm and joy. I was in candlelight, and incense sent a beautiful aroma into the room. Suddenly I felt a presence coming towards me. I stopped singing and listened inward with my senses and I became silent; "I am the light of the world" the power of the voice filled the entire room. It was as if I was enveloped in a Being. I knew that God was present, and when I heard the message, it came with a revelation. This happened instantly, and I understood the meaning; He is the light we see and the light we are all looking for, he/she *is* the light. This knowing flooded my being and I saw that light is knowledge, that is, total certainty of what is true. Darkness is the absence of this wisdom. Then I heard the voice again; "thou shalt have no other masters but me." I understood when the message came in that by seeking many truths, I had fragmented the power that came through me; I had become like a sieve. An image appeared and I saw myself pulling energies back to my center, and I felt how the power of the light became solidified. This new ability to focus had become a manifested presence. It is hard to explain in words, the feelings and certainty were just there. I saw how doubt and uncertainty fragmented the power coming through me.

I sank back into my chair. I had probably straightened up when I had heard the voice, my back was straight as a rod, and I had total attention. Again, I became conscious of the song, and the lyrics enveloped me. The words came out as if they were messages from eternity; *I must love this light, which comes from the divine. To be a child of it I must love from the heart. I must love the light from the heart.* The universe knows how to organise itself perfectly. A mixture of joy and seriousness abounded in my nervous system as I continued the songs. This love felt like champagne, it came like little rushing bubbles from a living river. Someone had popped the cork, or maybe Saint Michael did it with the top of his sword? I knew this was the decision I had to make; to be firm in my connection to God to stay on the ferry and cross over the river, as it was shown to me in my dream.

I had to decide where my focus was. This had to be a decision which honoured my values and united all my beliefs without being scattered in many directions. I knew that this would happen sooner or later, so why not sooner than later? The truth which I had discovered mirrored the truth I had experienced in 1991, I had no doubt. Jesus and Mary are always paying attention to my thoughts and actions; nothing is hidden, as shown in both dreams and visions. This is what I came here to do: find my way back to God. The light from God is what guides us and lights up the path, this is what Jesus tried to tell the world. I felt as if I was standing in the doorway to truth. I saw the road in front of me light up and it was a narrow path where darkness lurked on both sides.

Cleansing Fire

After I was given these insights, I felt that I had started 'life part three'. I felt that the reason for my being here became clearer every day, as if I were now allowed to take part in something that had been kept hidden from me. My power was contained in the light from God, and I experienced what Jesus said: "with the fruits the truth shall be known". Peace was what I experienced, and that is one of the good fruits from the tree. This feeling became a constant component in me. It wasn't just in my heart, it felt like every cell in my body *was at* peace. There were no fights anywhere, everything could be just as it was. I had known peace and love for a long time, but now it was as if a new dimension of it was revealing itself. All the gurus and awakened people talk of how their revelations cannot be expressed in words, only experienced. Now it became true to me, no words could describe what I saw and felt. I was part of a living stream, the one flowing through everyone and everything in my vision. How could I explain the memories popping up, the glimpses of different lives my soul contained? It was as when my higher self revealed the dna strands I studied in the vision, like I was waking up little by little.

The vision in one of my dreams, the one I had in Lima where I was shown the way into myself by searching first for myself, then directly for God, came clearly before me. Now I could understand more of what it wanted to say: only He can show me who I am, I can never *find* myself. God is the only one who can reveal to me who I am. If

I was searching, I would only find the created part playing different roles, the changeable. What *was* me had to be revealed. The story I had heard from Mooji several times now became so obvious. He was talking about the thief who works as a police officer, and when he comes to work his task is to catch the thief. He puts on his uniform and starts the hunt. Will he find the thief? I had to laugh; this is what we are doing here. How could the world get such a hold of us that we lost sight of who we are? Everything is visible, but still so hard to spot. When God's light shone on me, I saw in a glance who I am. I wanted to know why I had been hiding and why it was easier to turn away than to allow the light to show me the truth.

The suffering, the pain, the despair I had experienced, were nothing more than shadows I had been hiding behind. They had given me permission to be angry and to argue with life. My parents showed me the opposite of what I needed, and brought out the person who feared the world, it became a dangerous place. The little girl got caught in the spider's web, and I needed a long time to figure out how to get out of it. I could see how the story made me play out the opposite of what I longed for the most: love and acceptance. What I missed the most during childhood was being able to be me and to express my opinions. Step by step I opened myself up to *be* what I was longing for. The world was just a reflection of myself, I knew this, but I still had to bring forth the courage to break the patterns programmed deep inside.

On my way to visit my son and his dear family, I was left thinking about how life puts all the puzzle pieces perfectly together. I had a beautiful Greek daughter-in-law and was surprised at how at home I felt every time I visited their land. They had lived in London for many years but moved closer to her family after the pandemic spread. I was happy they now got support and help with two active boys, and I wanted to visit them as often as I could. Unfortunately, it wasn't easy due to quarantine rules, but now I was on my way to be with them during the holidays. They had rented a house by the sea not far from the island where they married some years back. I was really looking forward to seeing everyone again, the boys grew up so fast and I wanted them to get to know their Norwegian grandmother.

I sat looking out the window while my thoughts were drifting. The plane was almost empty, and it was an atmosphere of calm which I hadn't known on my travels before. Usually there was hectic activity with food trollies going back and forth, passengers chatting and laughing out loud to deafen the aircraft engine. Now it was quiet. The seats next to me were empty so the occasion was perfect to let my mind go its own way. I looked out and could see we were now crossing the Alps. Mountain peaks towered high and small dots indicated that people were living in the valley. I could see green grass glittering between the mountainsides, and I had to smile at the thoughts coming in: God is in everything, even in the environment I was looking at down there, the peaks where the sunshine made the snow sparkle, the valley resting in the shades of the mountains. Both were perfect images of this. My mind wandered by itself, sending images to my brain. The realisations I had had in the last two years had been transformative.

The pain we feel is also God's pain because he is in everything, that is why I felt the world's suffering in the vision, and in the dream where I channelled. The suffering is in God's embrace. Not a single small fragment escapes him because he is all there is. Now he keeps on calling all the parts of himself back to love. Lucifer, whom we call the ruler of the world, wants separation from God, which is the illusion we believe in. This energy will do what it can to pull us away from reaching into the core of remembering. When Jesus showed up in one of the visions, I saw how the crucifixion was the perfect image of the suffering we experience. He wanted to show us the truth he had found, because we had ended up so far from who we are that we no longer knew where to look. The sounds of the souls had been put to sleep, and the music of the cosmos is not complete without all the notes. The understanding of all that I had experienced rushed through me as we started the descent. The world far down there came closer, whilst my thoughts floated in the cosmos.

The world we live in doesn't want the light. We can talk about anything as long God or Jesus are not mentioned. Buddha, Shiva, Ganesha, Yogananda, Ramana Maharshi, Maharaj, all are welcomed and are received with open arms. They all provide great guidance in search of truth, and they all found what they were looking for. All of them have been important for me during my own search for answers. It was after the revelation that I became aware that Jesus is the only one who says, "I am the way, the truth, and the life." He pointed not at himself but towards the Father. I know that when we have a real desire to find an answer, we are guided to go exactly where we need to go. There are many enlightened people who help us find our way home, and I am extremely grateful for each one. I knew that the core in me would be revealed when every layer had been lit up, the onion had to be peeled until every hidden secret was revealed. The center of the onion consists of nothing, and this emptiness consists of everything. Love is the glue that binds all there is. It is not a physical substance we can see or touch, it is so light that it exists in everything, we just need to find it. The darkness wants to hide everything, leading us astray when we are on the right track. This is the task of the world. It is like a cat and mouse game that never ends, not until we can see through the game.

I have been visited in my dreams by several archetypal energies. Shiva and Ganesha came together in one, and Thoth showed up in another. When Shiva appeared, the feeling was a jumble of creation, like a rollercoaster in eternal ups and downs. When Ganesha arrived, I became aware of a huge strength and protection. While remembering this I was reminded of another dream which I had a few years ago.

214

I am in a big mansion. The walls are made of dark mahogany, and I am standing in a large hall. Along the hallway upstairs on the first floor, I see many doors leading into different rooms. The floor I am standing on is covered with a large thick Persian rug in deep red. The stairs leading up to the first floor are wide and are slightly curving towards the right. I know that there are other people in the house, but I cannot see anyone. Everything is quiet and I start walking up the stairs. The steps are covered by the same Persian rug, so my steps are muted. I am about to approach the first floor and notice a door that stands ajar. Carefully I go over and peek inside. I see shelf upon shelf loaded with beautiful figures, all the shelves are full of them. They resemble statues sold around the world; treasures collected by generations on their travels. I recognise Buddha, Shiva, and Ganesha. There are countless others in a row, some are black as ebony, while others are gold-plated or wooden.

Carefully I walk around while I study them all. Surprisingly I see flames begin to lick around each and everyone. I understand that I need to leave the room and close the door after me. The door needs to be kept closed while the figures are burning, if it is opened prematurely the entire room will burn down. I know that I am there to be a doorman, that is why I came. When I close it, I can see small windows in the door, they are handmade and have recessed glass panes. This makes it possible to follow what is happening inside the room. People rush towards me asking to go in. I reply that they must wait and I explain what is going on. They look in and see flames licking around the figures, then they move on.

They are burning for quite a while, and people come and go. Eventually the flames subside, and I see that the fires have burned out. I open the door to go inside and the smell of smoke left from the fires is intense. I quickly walk over to the large windows on the other side of the room to open them. A fresh breeze rushes in and makes the white, light curtains flutter in the wind. The smell of grass and flowers surround me, and I take a deep breath. The smell of smoke disappears, *it is as if the energy in the room has changed. Now it feels light and has a beautiful scent of flower meadows. The shelves are empty, and the heavy energy has disappeared, I didn't notice the heavy energy before it was gone. I look out of the window, admiring the view of the beautiful park surrounding the mansion.*

Every time it popped into my memory, I wondered what it really wanted to tell me. Now the message was clear: all the stories and memories we hang on to are weighing us down. When we collect old treasures, the dust that accumulates, the energy they possess, will keep us trapped. They become like threads in a spider's web. By letting everything go, like the pillow I was holding in front of me, the energy can flow freely. The memories will still be there, but they no longer have roots that make us stuck. We are free. The world could no longer get hold of me, I had pulled up the roots. The flames burning up all the receptors got rid of the negative forces where emotions could be attached to me. By letting go of all the old beliefs, I had said yes to what was real and no to the world's perceptions. The ease I felt in the dream cannot be described in words. It was like the fresh breeze was leading all the scents in. When I accepted the wedding ring, the same feeling entered me. I could now see how the dreams had guided me all my life. Here, where we are cut off from the recollection of who and what we are, where we come from, we need help. This help is always there, but it can take time to understand how it speaks to us.

The plane taxied towards the terminal, and the world entered through the window. The blue sky, the tranquility up there, had been replaced by frantic activity. I was looking forward to seeing them all again, it had been several months since the last time I was in Greece. The feeling of being in transit made me smile, I still had to sit still, the plane hadn't arrived, while the hustle and bustle of the world was right outside. The dream about the cars that weighed down on me, came into me as knowledge: They represented all the lives that I contained, all the ancestors, all generations forward and backward were parts of this self, and when I returned home, I simultaneously took all of them with me. The truth I had found was interconnected with everyone. This became very clear after seeing the dna threads floating around the center. Every time I lingered on that vision, it was as if new dimensions and remembrances opened. When I found the center, the driving force, the power that gives life to this self, then the power and wisdom will spread out into all the dna threads and dissolve the magnet which was trying to drag me down in frequency.

I stepped out into the warm Greek air, finally I was here again. The wind rushed through my hair while I found the taxi driver they had ordered for me. Here nothing was left to chance. The thoughtfulness they always showed gave me a sense of being cared for, being loved. Her whole family had welcomed us with open arms, and we were always welcome as they are with us. And the olive oil... I was already looking forward to dipping bread into it, nothing tastes better than the Greek olive oil. Well, maybe moussaka, I had to have moussaka before I went back home too.

Karma

More and more I was immersed in revelations which came directly from the light, the very light that shone upon what had been hidden in the dark. After the focus was centered in me, in my core, it was as if the force was increasing. What was almost visible in the past now came in with full certainty. By allowing the blinkers to dissolve I became open to what the world didn't want me to see. Again, I received confirmation that God is bringing all parts of himself back into love. The ego, the created individual who believe it is separated from God, was so clear. How is it possible not to see this? How could the world's view become so strong that I believed more in what *it* told me than what the voice inside tried to say? By making visible how I clung to my own blinkers, I understood that this was my own creation. I had made the choices, stubborn as a mare, I was going to do this myself in my own way. Cycle after cycle I returned to correct my tendency to turn my back on God, each time trapped in the ego's creation of itself, believing in the fears the world wanted me to hold on to. I ended up in the spider's web again and again.

The image of people running here and there in complete confusion came clearly before me. Here I saw how the demands of the world were the yardstick. We degraded ourselves when we didn't fulfil the wishes of the world, without realising what we were doing. I remembered how ridiculously idiotic this looked when I saw it from outside. We dug our own grave as we listened to the world, removing ourselves more and more from who we really are. The soul didn't let go, I knew it was waiting for me to discover the essence of myself, to give up the mirror I had been looking into. The dream I had where I was shown how time is created in the brain had been important. I needed to understand that it was just a concept and not the truth. Knowledge acquired through the intellect was constantly changing, while the wisdom outside of time was immutable. The whole world existed with time as a basis, without time religions would not have been able to survive. They needed a story to tell.

The priests claim that we end up in hell if we do not abide by the laws and rituals that they have created. We *live* in hell, it is absence of God, of contact with our own soul. Religions keep us away from the core by twisting the words to their advantage. Fear is the best means of gaining power over someone, when we are in fear the energy is pulled out of us. Hell is the dark spot I saw in the dream; it is the row of windows that I saw spiralling downwards into earth in another dream. Ever since Jesus had been physically present, he had been laughed at, the priests and Pharisees started crusades during which many lives were sacrificed. The Inquisition forced the people into a faith which *they* had created, and they killed anyone who refused. They even killed Jesus. The Ten Commandments are something the priests talked about, but did not follow themselves, or are even following now. The world is the domain we enter, where the memory and remembrance of who we are is covered. It is so easy to follow the laws of our community when our inner voice is put to sleep.

The resistance to acknowledging Jesus's words had been deeply rooted in me as well. The layers needing to be removed have been many, and I did not capitulate until he came and showed me the significance of the crucifixion. What came in as a knowing when I looked at the cross, was our belief that the body is what we are. When we 'nail' ourselves to the body, the suffering is a fact. Then we are convinced that we are the body and that the story is who we are.

It is only through liberation of the belief of being the body that we can be set free from pain. If we are an eternal soul and not a limited body, the story cannot be true either. The story is an experience, but it doesn't identify the totality of who I am. It shapes my identity, but I am so much more. The pain is inside the story, so when I no longer identify with it, it must dissolve.

I am sitting inside the little church where my son and daughter-in-law were married. It is so simple, so free of gold and glitter, and there is maybe room for twenty people here. The benches are made of wood, aged by the ravages of time. I looked around at white brick walls. A few reliefs struck a note in my heart, and a beautiful candelabra was standing ready to be lit on the altar in front of me. Outside the heat was shimmering, but inside it was cool. The energy was strong. Thoughts of the event that took place several years back made me smile. It had been a proper Mamma Mia wedding with two-hundred-and-fifty guests from far and wide. Friends and family from both sides had come to attend the union between my son and his love. Everything was going on outside, but this little church was the center. An old woman and her daughter had designated themselves as the church's protectors, they were caring for it with loving hands. I had just spoken to them with a few words of English and gesturing, and I was able to make them understand that I wanted to enter. The old woman smiled and showed a few teeth, her eyes sparkling with love for this beautiful little building, a black headscarf covered most of her hair to protect her head from the radiating sun.

As I looked around, I came to think of my first trip to Greece. It had happened many years ago, long before my kids were partners. I experienced something inexplicable that I had wondered about many times, and what the incident was showing to me. We were five couples who had agreed to go on vacation together, to one of the beautiful islands Greece can boast of. One day we decided to explore the island and we rented two cars. On that day we arrived at a picturesque little village at noon, and we decided to stop and have lunch. The city was situated on a mountain hill with a breathtaking panoramic view of the Mediterranean. All the streets were narrow, with alleys and small intimate taverns. We wanted to find a place where we could enjoy the view, and eventually found a cozy restaurant. When we looked in, we could see straight through large windows, and the Mediterranean Sea was sparkling in the sun far below. Everyone went straight out onto the balcony, and I was the last person out. It was so narrow, there was just room for small tables with one chair on each side. The view was obscured by the others until I stepped out, and I looked straight down into a gorge. I began to hyperventilate, my legs trembled, and I felt my whole body begin to shiver. Fear of heights had never been an issue, it washed over me by surprise.

I almost ran inside whilst my tears were running down my cheeks. There was no way to stop the reaction, it came like a bolt of lightning. I shivered like a leaf and sat down concentrating on breathing calmly. It took me a long time before I was able to gather myself enough to give an explanation. They had never seen me in such a condition, and I had never been in one like this either. They were in total confusion and just looked at me with a lot of questions in their eyes. There and then I understood as little as they did, but I was able to tell them that I had a panic attack when I looked down the ravine. Many years later I discovered I had had a life in Greece, which ended off a cliff. When this life showed up, I remembered the incident, it popped out from the drawer where I had stored the experience.

The life it came from was a past life where I was a seer. My job was to communicate with the scholars and tell them what was best to do regarding a situation, and to tell them what was coming. In the beginning I was proud to be asked, there was a kind of power in it. Eventually, however, I understood how they used what I had conveyed against the people. The resistance to saying what they wanted to hear grew, and in the end, I refused to say anything. Then they made the process short and pushed me off the cliff. Kind of funny we were now connected to this country. Photos taken from the wedding abounded with orbs, as if all the ancestors had come to celebrate. I got a feeling this was exactly as had been planned, our connection had been restored.

No wonder that I felt at home in this environment, our karmic connection was strong. My thoughts went to the first time we visited my daughter-in-law's family. We went to the Acropolis whilst the heat stood shimmering around us. The sun was shining in an azure blue sky as we climbed steep, old stone stairs. As we progressed, I felt the energies increase. My daughter, who was with us, experienced the same feeling, and we both walked like sleepwalkers around the old buildings. On one occasion she waved me to come, and asked if I could walk around a bit and find an area with a lot of energy. I strolled around and walked over to a side entrance of one of the temples. A sea of energy approached me, and I called her. "You found exactly the same spot as me." she wasn't surprised, she just wanted confirmation. The energy was so powerful it was almost like a portal back to the time this was a living place. It was like I was walking in old memories, but these came as feelings and not as pictures. Today I might have been able to get a handle on where this energy came from, but it was a positive feeling of something familiar. As we went downstairs to find a shady place to have lunch, she chose to stay behind. She couldn't tear herself away and wanted to walk around alone for a while.

My thoughts wandered by themselves. There was a huge peace in the little church, a silence that would be broken as soon as I opened the door and stepped outside. The world out there felt so far away in the stillness of the room. Although nothing surprised me anymore, it was amazing how my life had designed itself. My intentions and thoughts were the creators of what I needed to do. The law of cause and effect always applied, even from one life to another. What we sow, we will reap. All experiences are in the soul. The horror I experienced by being pushed off the cliff, my regret at contributing to people having a hard time, this I had to sort out. Although it happened in the 1700s, the energy was alive. It was kept as a memory stuck in the soul; an aspect frozen in time. I looked up at the wooden cross hanging on the wall right in front of me, and I felt an energy tingling in my skin. An old dream came sailing in with it, a dream I had had when I was seventeen years old which I had never written down, but it was like I was sitting in a movie theatre looking at a screen, and the dream was as clear now as when it first appeared.

I become aware that I am on my way up a simple wooden staircase. It leads up onto a stage and the crowd stands close by. My hands are tied behind my back, and I am pushed up by someone behind me. The dress I wear is red and shows a higher rank than the people who have crowded together. It is dirty, as though I have had it on for days. My red hair is flowing down my back. I am pushed over to a guillotine that is ready and I put my head and hands in the recesses. These get locked by a wooden bar, and I see that the executioner is getting ready. The crowd that has come to watch what is about to happen is completely silent, as he grips the cord which is linked to the axe blade. The moment that he pulls the line I move up and away from the body. I observe how the axe parts the head from the body, and how the head falls into a basket. The executioner bends down, grabs the head, and lifts it up by the hair. I can see the head dangling at the end of it. I am woken by the cheers of the crowd.

Many of the stories that we carry with us are grotesque; no wonder peace is absent. "You too, Jesus, were crucified." I look up at the simple cross on the wall, which is the evidence of how cruel humanity can be. "Forgive them, for they do not know what they are doing." He saw what karma they were creating for themselves, and his words came from love and truth. The image of myself moving out of my body before the pain came about was proof that my body wasn't me. I became an observer. What was happening down there had nothing to do with me, it was just a movie. The body that I saw could have been a wax figure. "When someone hits you on your right cheek, turn the left." Simple rules that Jesus had tried to teach, so that we wouldn't get caught in the eternal cycle of karma, thereby creating more suffering in our next incarnation.

Now, I could understand what he meant. Everyone who had caused me pain had been operating out of their own suffering. They were living in their own survival mode, believing the world was the only truth, where the right of the privileged applied, and we are allowed to tread on corpses to reach our goals. How easy life could be if we could only live by the rules that Jesus told us. I had experienced how much easier it was when I released my story and no longer was in anger or hate. Now that I didn't hold my parents accountable for my life, I got back into the power to create what I wanted. The strange thing is that the more I forgave the more benefit came into sight, the negative spiral started to go upwards instead of downwards. When I feared the world, it had to confirm my beliefs, and more suffering entered. When love and gratitude took over it gave me confirmation of this too. When my perception changed my world changed.

Karma is nothing more than the law of cause and effect. The love I experienced in 1991 held nothing against anyone. It is the ego that keeps our neighbour responsible for the life we have created, we judge everyone else and thus ourselves. Why is it so difficult to see what we are doing to ourselves? Where I was sitting in deep peace, everything became simple and self-sufficient. I went up and gave thanks for the moment inside this nice little church room, it was as if the simple white walls in the church invited purity. Without the gold and glitter everything seemed so simple, I didn't need anything. When I stepped outside, the old woman was removing withered leaves in the flowerbed along the wall. I went over to give thanks for the moment, and her daughter came over to translate. When I mentioned the good energy, she smiled and thanked me. "It is through people like you the good energy is there." The answer surprised me, it was the last thing that I had expected to hear. Thoughtfully I strolled towards the stone fence surrounding the church appreciating her great wisdom.

The olive trees abounded with fruit, and I had to stop and admire them. These trees are one of the most beautiful trees I know. It is like they keep the memories of generations, and the trunk is like a work of art, no two are alike. The branches spread outwards in beautiful formations, providing lovely shades on hot summer days. You guys are happy here too, I had to smile as I studied some olives who were about to get their deep magenta colour before I strolled on to the stone fence and sat down. There I could see down the mountainside, steeply down to the water. A fishing boat was on its way in to deliver his morning's catch. The fear of heights never returned.

I could still hear the old woman's words in my ear; it is the energy we leave behind us that stores itself in the walls. What if we could send love wherever we went? Many places had made me feel uncomfortable previously, it was just a matter of getting away from there, now I just registered the negative energies. The aura surrounding us contains everything which the soul wants us to heal. Once the job is done, we can breathe more freely, and receptors where negative energy used to attach, won't be able to. It was good to notice that nothing was activated in me anymore, at least very rarely. Now I just recorded it, listened in, and didn't have to act. How liberating to live free of encumbrances. I got up from the lookout area and I slowly strolled down the road which was winding down the mountainside, the same road the bride and groom had walked, accompanied by beautiful music as they approached the beach where all the guests were waiting on the day my son and daughter-in-law got married. Now two children, my beautiful grandchildren, were waiting for me.

The Awakening

The book I had been writing for a couple of months was coming to an end, I felt it in every fibre of my body. The journey writing this book was bigger and deeper than I could have ever imagined. From the threads entwining together I could see clearly how the tissues of life brought in all the ingredients for me to understand. The programmes that were inculcated in my brain from childhood, and stayed with me through time, had been the engine that held everything together, creating what became my identity. The dreams, visions, and all the downloads I had received, were parts arising from the depths of my soul and into my consciousness. By listening to them and respecting the messages that they had brought in, they were able to unfold, it is so easy to dismiss new thoughts as fantasy or that they are impossible to follow. Now I know that what does not already exist in a frequency, or a dimension, is not possible for us to imagine. Images, thoughts, and ideas come from the rich library of the universe. When we set a goal, and we imagine what it is going to be like, we are climbing up in frequencies; it is like Jacob's ladder. When we achieve a goal, we reach a higher vibration. My goal had been clear since the experience which I had had in 1991. I had to find love, beyond sensations of pain, and behind all the difficult experiences my soul was carrying. I was homesick, without being conscious of what I was longing for.

Occasionally my experience of what happened on the steps of the church house, would come sailing in. There I was standing outside the building without the presence of myself, all my feelings were absent. It had been a surprising incident. Right there and then I couldn't understand what was happening, I had no knowledge of who I was. Now I know that I was being shown what it was like to exist without contact with my soul. Life had given me many wounds, and I continued to shut down parts of me. The result could have been total shutdown from origin, from God. What I experienced was the existence of man without his soul. When we shut off the inner voice, we allow the ego, the created part, to take over. My intellect and rational thoughts can work without the participation of my essence, which is the immortal part. Then we will have no contact with our empathy or feelings, which is what helps us interact with others or to navigate the physical environment. The laws of the world will then be the only thing that applies, where the riches become supreme. This is the created human being, the identity we become through the environment surrounding us growing up. Love and the desire to do good for others is not present here, the survival instinct becomes paramount. Love and compassion are found when we have contact with ourselves, with the soul. When the inner voice is squeezed away in favour of fear, uncertainty and doubt, parts of our soul cannot get through. Then we start living in separation, because of the polarity in which we experience the world. The journey we have chosen to do in the physical world is to learn how to listen to the voice of the soul, rather than the world's opinions. This is the path of awakening.

Before I completed the writing, I wanted to go out into the woods and contemplate, and to feel into if my guides had more on their minds. It was a beautiful late summer day, the sun shone warmly and deliciously against my skin, the heatwave was over, and a dash of autumn could be sensed in the air. It made me think about the trips in the woods we used to take when the children were small.

Red, juicy cranberries between deep-green leaves; good memories that made me smile. Now they had children of their own, with whom they made their memories. I sniffed the warm scent of the earth as I strolled down to the stump, my favourite spot where the forest behind felt like a shawl around my shoulders. The sea washing against the pebbles in front of me was making my gaze travel endlessly.

I gazed in silence and enjoyed the scents and sounds around me. The leaves of the trees rustled gently in the breeze, and I noticed that the beach cabbage between the rocks had been de-flowered. They sent a little whine as if they wanted contact and to make themselves visible, I smiled at them whilst listening inwardly. It was quiet. A butterfly sat on my knee, a small creature with white wings and fragile, light grey veins glittering in the sunlight. Its wings fluttered in tender twitches, as it peeked at me, it was as if it welcomed me out of the cocoon, now we were both free. What had shut us up as we grew in strength, had been a gift from mother nature. We needed the time of struggle to be able to fly high. The barriers of resistance which we had been through were only the beginning, I could see that now. The walls of the cocoon, all the limitations were supposed to be there, as we pressed against what stopped the unfolding, the space getting narrower the more I grew. Eventually the clearings between the cracks became visible, giving me courage to keep going, increasing the strength to push further. Now the walls were gone.

A steel worm quickly slid between the rocks, and I had to smile at the thought of the fear which they had raised in me earlier. The walks in the jungle had cured so much, more than I could ever have dreamed about. Now I saw their beauty and knew that they too are perfectly designed, the ecosystem must work for us to exist in physical life. Nothing is accidental. "The flowers in the field do not worry." This simple statement said so much, and it took me so long to understand the depths of what its meaning was. When we no longer worry, we are free, worrying comes from old programming and it obscures the present. When we leave the present moment, we start to believe that the story we tell ourselves are truth. That is the link to the challenges of the past, and we might recreate the past once again. The cycle of nature has a lot to teach us. The tree releases its leaves when its time for rest has come, it does not protest or cling to what was. Our thoughts complicate everyday life, bouncing back and forth non-stop, causing our adrenaline to increase. Herein lies the stress.

A sailboat appeared on the horizon, and I saw how the breeze against my own face filled the sails far out there, as if playing with the wind. Imagine if we could let the breeze of life bring us home without resistance and fear. How simple life could be when the inner voice of the soul was in command: this is what is called waking up. I let the inner images unfold freely, feeling the eternal presence surround me, what, how and when no longer existed. All the questions which had started my journey had been answered. How this quest would bring me to where I am today, I could never have imagined. Everything is now, I felt joy ripple through me like a river, the realisation was deep. The words from a beautiful girl I had got to know during my travels, came sailing in: "you don't have to hold on to everything you know, just let it come when you need it."

I remembered how tears of relief had made my eyes shine as the understanding sank in, it was as if the weight on my shoulders fell off. Everything I thought I had to hold on to disappeared in an instant. The depths of what she had said gradually emerged, as the layers which I had held on to were transformed and expanded. Just by letting go of everything I was free, like the pillow in that dream. I had to be light as a feather. What I needed would always come at the right time, in the moment that it was needed. I have experienced this truth in so many ways, when I listened from my heart, what was needed came along by itself. It came from eternity, from the contact of the soul. It wants us to find home and it guides us every second of the time we are in the physical, life after life, all we need is to listen into the silence; so simple, and yet so difficult.

The butterfly rubbed its front legs against each other, waving its wings, getting ready to continue its journey. I smiled at it in gratitude. The gift of the little being came directly from the source of life, and the love felt like an eternal stream. This is what I am, what I come from and go back to. Now I know how much I am loved. Do you?

EPILOGUE

Writing this book has taught me so much. The perspective became visible as I tried to draw a chronological line. The threads came to light as the dreams and visions appeared when I wrote. The magic web of life, with all its colours and images, is so clear through the words that came through. I see how everything has guided me safely and securely, going forward even when I didn't feel safe, or knew where to go. Everything happening, all the ups and downs, was just a story I was going through. "It is through suffering that we find home, and you are the one that has chosen your life." How many times have I not read and heard these words, shaking my head in denial. I could never *have chosen* this myself, could I? Now I could see the connection, without the pain I wouldn't have found myself. I may not have chosen the inner path if life had been a dance in pleasure. The outside, the world, would have been enough for me.

God's love flooding through was the catalyst which I needed. It pointed to the path I was looking for. What I was shown I could not have begun to understand from the consciousness which I had had at the time. I had to take the journey of dropping all my belief systems, one by one. All my life I had been guided to do this work. Although guides showed up in my dreams, I had failed to understand how close they were to me before it was shown to me in the vision. Only then did I manage to understand they were inside me as close as my breath, it was my own despair and disbelief which was preventing contact.

As human beings we live life in fear of death; what exists to us on the outside, is all that exists. If our focus is maintained in this belief, if that becomes the truth; living from this perspective life will be dangerous. The only thing we know is that when we are born, we will die. Therefore, to hold on to life, we must fight decay for as long as possible, which has made many people rich just by 'helping' people to stay young as long as possible. These are battles which we are doomed to lose, our bodies are going back to mother earth no matter what we do. If we look out to the world and believe this to be all there is, we will come into hardship, the oblivion of who we are uses all means to keep us in this conviction. We are pleased with small glimpses of happiness, and we believe that this is how it is. It is all about proving to each other that we are good enough, and we fight to have what others around us possess, plus more to show off. It is weighed and measured, and the ego's definition of justice becomes the prevailing law. We live life on the outside as if that is the only thing there is. It brings us into a life of constant change and uncertainty, of ups and downs.

The vision that came to me in Lima, when God showed me the path to find myself, has become truth for me. Today I am in no doubt. When Jesus came and showed me the meaning of the crucifixion, I saw many lives where I had tried to escape from God. By acknowledging the truth of what I was shown, and by asking for forgiveness, I became whole again. Here I could see the world from a completely different angle. It became revealed to me when I understood the eternal, that which does not change. It was like the story of the seeds that were spread around by the wind, some ending up on mountains, where the roots they grew became shallow. When the autumn storm comes, the plant is torn up. Those who end up among thistles are swallowed by the weeds, and have a difficult upbringing, most of them die before they reach full growth. Only those who end up in good soil, will grow up and become the plants that they were meant to be, strong, healthy, and straight. When looking back I could see the strength and wisdom my story had given to me. This would not have been visible without the light of truth, the light of love. It is as if I have been in a maturing process, which exploded when the sun's rays were directed at it. Now I can remember what was previously hidden. As the vision had shown to me, I would find myself immediately when I found God, as I am created *in* God energy.

In the process of healing the pain which my soul had contained, I would need a lot of time alone. Every layer peeling off brought me closer to myself, all those times I was feeling my way into something, but it was still diffuse. I was constantly listening inward; my own time had to be prioritised, I had to choose me. This was not possible before, or I would have felt a lot of guilt if I prioritised myself. Now I know that guilt arises from old programming which keeps me away from myself. Had I been a more social person, involved in everything life could offer, the world would have continued to pull me outside of myself, contributing to my uncertainty. By being with myself I could choose what I wanted to listen to, contemplate and feel what was right. I had time to grow strong, just like the butterfly when it is transformed in the chrysalis.

After I started to write this book, I began a new journey. I had thought that the notes would be my supervisors, and I had put aside many notes. Events, dreams, reflections, and inner experiences, which I had documented, had been laid aside chronologically, ready to be used. It didn't turn out that way. All the pages were left in the binder, the words came by themselves. The dreams appeared without my having any idea that they were going to be a part of the book, dreams, and events which I had forgotten became alive in front of me. Being so personal wasn't on my agenda when I first started writing, I have never been as open as here and now. This had brought out my anxiety of exposing myself. What if people judged me? What if no one wanted to be friends with me anymore? All thoughts which activate fear do not come from the truth, I knew that I must test myself once more. Which was the most important - was it the world or the truth which I had discovered?

I was looking at the choice which was clearly in front me, and I had no doubt. The world could never give me what I have been missing, the fullness of love and the totality of the soul. I can live here, but I am no longer own by this world, nor is the fear of what it can do to me significant any longer. Other people's thoughts are not of my concern, I must just listen to what my own heart is telling me. I am one with God, with the source of life, and His/Her words and laws are what I want to participate within. Here I find everything which I will always need. For several years I have felt a need to write, as if the book must be written. This challenged me since I am an introverted person. Now I see that my fear of being fully immersed, has helped me to create a division on my inside; I had been living with one version of me showing to the outside, and another version of myself facing inwards.

My last husband would often say, "you will never get my thoughts," and I wondered what was so important for him to keep hidden. Now I know that hiding is just an illusion which we surround ourselves with. If we can't be open, be who we are, we don't live in truth. My inner self must become visible outwards, only then am I living my life fully and whole. To get to this point I had needed to go through the process of releasing my own blinkers and my self-imposed limitations. I had to look my fear straight in the eye, and trust my inner guidance, my inner voice, and step out of my comfort zone. As a child, my father's words and opinions were the law I must abide by. That was the life I was going to experience at the beginning of this journey. Now I could continue my magical creation of the world in which I lived in, free to be me.

Milton Keynes UK
Ingram Content Group UK Ltd.
UKHW022232280324
440175UK00017B/1203